"Ooh." Her head fell back, exposing her long neck.

Hylan recognized an invitation when he saw one and leaned down to plant kisses on the line of her jaw all the way down to her sensitive collarbone. Kissing her was like finding the golden ticket to the chocolate factory. She tasted that damn sweet. What he really longed for was the taste of her caramel-tipped nipples. So much so that his stomach growled with hunger.

Nikki was lost in the magic that Hylan was creating. As for that little pesky voice in the back of her head, she'd gagged it and locked it in the deep recesses of her mind. All she wanted was for Hylan to keep doing what he was doing. She'd think about the consequences later. She sighed when Hylan's lips moved away from her neck then started to dip down the center of her body.

He was already the best she'd ever had because she'd never been with a man who'd even bothered with foreplay. Mindlessly, she ran her hand through his short cropped hair and then down his steely shoulders and onto the hard planes of his back. Lord, he had an incredible body.

Books by Adrianne Byrd

Kimani Romance

She's My Baby
When Valentines Collide
To Love a Stranger
Two Grooms and a Wedding
Her Lover's Legacy
Sinful Chocolate
*Tender to His Touch
Body Heat

*Hollington Homecoming

ADRIANNE BYRD

is a national bestselling author who has always preferred to live within the realms of her imagination, where all the men are gorgeous and the women are worth whatever trouble they manage to get into. As an army brat, Adrianne traveled throughout Europe and learned to appreciate and value different cultures. Now she calls Georgia home.

Ms. Byrd has been featured in many national publications, including *Today's Black Woman, Upscale* and *Heart and Soul.* She has also won local awards for screenwriting.

In 2006 Adrianne Byrd forged into the world of Street Lit as De'nesha Diamond. In 2008 she jumped into the young-adult arena, writing as A.J. Byrd, and this year Adrianne will hit the women's fiction scene as Layla Jordan. She plans to continue creating characters that make people smile, laugh and fall in love.

Body HEAT

Adrianne Byrd

KIMANI ROMANCE

Thanks to all my friends and fans who encourage me
every day to keep going.

KIMANI PRESS™

Recycling programs
for this product may
not exist in your area.

ISBN-13: 978-0-373-86168-2

BODY HEAT

www.kimanipress.com

Printed in U.S.A.

Dear Reader,

I hope that you enjoy *Body Heat,* part of the HEARTS-AT-PLAY GETAWAY series. Hylan and Nikki were fun characters to write and gave me the chance to indulge my penchant for romantic comedy.

The idea for this story just popped into my head one day. It's a fun spin on the secret-marriage storyline that is a staple of romance novels. I also loved the idea of creating a woman like Nikki, who has the best of intentions but never really thinks things through all the way.

In addition to being part of the GETAWAY series, this is the third book in my KAPPA PSI KAPPA series. I hope you've checked out the first two books: *Two Grooms and a Wedding* and *Sinful Chocolate.* The fun never stops with these fine frat brothers. In the previous KAPPA PSI KAPPA novels, Hylan was always perfect though we didn't really know too much about him. I hope his charm and ability to live in the moment win you over.

After reading *Body Heat* I hope you will visit and drop me a line at my Web site, www.adriannebyrd.com, or check me out on Facebook.

Happy reading,

Adrianne

Hylan Dawson is married.
The only problem is...no one bothered to tell him.

Chapter 1

"Places, everyone. Places!" Nicole Jamison shouted and clapped her hands to make sure she grabbed her small cast and crew's attention. "Five minutes 'til show time." Judging by the looks on their faces they were just as nervous about their opening night performance as she was. It was the *good* kind of nervous jitters—at least that's what she kept telling herself every five seconds.

Nicole smiled although every muscle in her stomach was now successfully tied into knots. This was it, the culmination of all of the blood, sweat and tears she'd put into her work for the past five years. Her first Broadway play!

Well, more like off-off-*off*-Broadway—but hell, it still counted. A year ago things were different. Her script, *Hot Comb and Hair Grease,* was all the buzz.

She and her agent enjoyed the highs and lows of a bidding war over the script. Investors were all lined up to launch Nikki's once dead-in-the-water career into the stratosphere.

No more ramen noodles for dinner.

No more battling mice and roaches for apartment space.

Most importantly—no more asking her parents for money.

Nikki, however, had underestimated her lifelong run of bad luck. In one fell swoop the bottom dropped out of the economy. Producers rescinded their offers, investors vanished into thin air and then her agent-slash-*best friend* flat out stopped returning her calls. The only things left were the ramen noodles, the mice and her parents' constant looks of disappointment and *their* checkbook.

What followed was a month long marathon of *The Oprah Winfrey Show: 20th Anniversary Collection* DVD. At first it was sad—no, it was still sad—but what emerged was a new attitude. Nikki, with Oprah's help, convinced herself that she didn't have to just accept this reality kick in the teeth. She could pick herself up, dust herself off and go about the business of turning this whole thing around. That's when the *brilliant* idea to produce the play herself emerged.

No. It was more like an epiphany—or as Oprah would say, an aha! moment—replete with a choir of angels singing in her head. And the more she thought about it, the more it made perfect sense. Everyone had loved the story once, right? So they would love it again.

All she needed was a good word-of-mouth campaign and she would be right back on top.

Problem solved.

Well, not quite. She also needed some money.

So Nikki emptied her savings account, which was enough to perhaps buy a pair of Payless shoes. Next, she convinced her parents to invest a good chunk of their retirement money in the production. It wasn't easy. Her father laughed for about three weeks and then when he realized that she was serious, he started treating her like she had the plague.

Typical.

Nikki then focused on her soft-hearted mother like a laser beam…and got a check from her. Okay, so it wasn't a very big check, but it was enough to lease a low-rent, rat-infested theater and buy a few costumes at the Salvation Army. The actors were the only thing that didn't cost money. In New York, out-of-work actors were a dime a dozen and they were willing to perform for the bare minimum: coffee.

Nikki pulled back the stage curtain and stole a quick peek at the front row. Her mom, beautiful in a cream-colored linen dress—usually reserved for Sunday morning church service—beamed with pride while her humorless father sat ramrod straight in a pair of basic brown khakis and a sky-blue open collar dress shirt. If he was excited about his daughter's opening night, it certainly didn't show.

Too many times her father had urged her to give up this whole writing thing and get a *real* job. Not that she hadn't tried. She had been everything from a waitress at a café to a much-maligned bill collector in order to pay her bills. What her parents and most of her friends failed to understand was that writing was her bliss. It was what she was born to do.

And tonight was her chance to prove it to the world, share her art, and let the New York theater community know that NICOLE JAMISON HAS ARRIVED.

Nikki drew a deep breath as a bright smile blossomed across her face, while her heart pounded like a race-horse.

"Nikki. Nikki."

Nicole whipped her head around to see Crystal Cummings, rushing toward her. Alarm bells immediately went off in Nicole's head when she saw her lead actress's face quickly turning puke-green.

Definitely not a good sign.

"Crystal, what is it?" Even as the question left her lips, Nikki's heart sank in anticipation of bad news. What would her life be without bad news?

"I can't—I can't go on." Crystal slapped a hand over her mouth just as a gagging, gurgling, chugging noise rose from her throat. Next, Crystal's large brown eyes bulged before she took off like a shot toward a plastic garbage can by the small buffet table.

The other actors scattered out of the way, but the sound of Crystal vomiting had a domino effect, causing a few more actors to turn green. That was the beauty of throwing up—either the sound or smell was all it took to spark a real outbreak.

"No. No. No." Nikki covered a hand over her heart as if that was going to stop everything from falling apart. It took a few more seconds for her to realize that she needed to *do* something. She rushed over to the garbage can and held Crystal's long wavy hair away from her face. It was the least she could do. But the stench wafting from the trash can now had the knots in Nikki's stomach flopping around.

The understudy. Nikki's gaze whipped around as she looked backstage for Crystal's understudy. "Where's Grace?" she shouted, but her question was met with blank stares from the other actors. Then she caught a quick glimpse out of the corner of her eyes. "Grace!"

The woman froze.

A second set of alarm bells went off when she noticed Grace looked like a deer caught in headlights. Definitely another bad sign.

Nikki released Crystal's hair and raced over to Grace. "You're gonna have to go on tonight." She may as well have told the understudy that she had terminal cancer from the look of sheer horror that blanketed Grace's face.

"I can't. I can't." Grace stepped back until her small frame was pressed against the back wall.

"What do you mean?" Nikki grabbed the young, pencil-thin actress by the shoulders, but then reminded herself at the last second that it was illegal to snap the woman in half. "We don't have a choice. You *have* to go on."

"B-But I didn't learn the lines," she confessed in a high-pitched whine.

"What?" Nikki's heart sank deeper in the pit of her

stomach. "What do you mean you *didn't* learn the lines? You're Crystal's understudy."

"I know…. But Crystal is such a good actress I didn't think anything could go wrong. Not to mention my college courses are really kicking my ass this quarter and my boyfriend and I have been fighting and—"

"Grace! Focus!"

The young understudy snapped her jaw shut. But then Grace's eyes started blinking so much, Nikki was afraid that she was in the middle of an epileptic fit.

"The bottom line is that you didn't bother to learn your lines," Nikki said, feeling as if the floor was spinning beneath her feet. "I don't believe this. In a few minutes I'm about to be the biggest joke on Broadway."

"You mean *off-off*-Broadway," Grace corrected.

Nikki's eyes narrowed. "Don't push it. You're already on my bad side."

Grace teared up. "I'm really, *really* sorry." And with that weak-ass apology, she scampered off.

"Curtain in two minutes," Barbara, Nikki's stage manager-slash-assistant-slash-baby sister, announced as if everything was all sunshine and roses.

Barbara caught sight of Nikki's horror-stricken face and rushed right over. "What's wrong?"

"I don't have a lead actress," Nikki choked out. She checked over her shoulder to see Crystal still hunched over the garbage can and dry heaving into it. "You don't happen to have a gun on you, do you?"

Barbara steered her sister's attention away from the sick actress. "C'mon now. She's not worth it."

"It's not for her. It's for me. I'd rather do myself in than have the critics do it."

"C'mon. It's not like Ben Brantley is out there."

"Please. Who needs *The New York Times* when you have this little bitty thing called the Internet?"

The desperation of the situation seemed to finally hit Barbara because she clammed up for a few seconds. "But what about—?"

"She didn't learn her lines," Nikki answered in a flat tone. "An understudy that doesn't study…." She smacked her palm against her forehead—which seemed to flip the switch on a lightbulb. Nikki looked at her sister with renewed hope.

Barbara's eyes bulged as she inched away. "Don't look at me. I'm not an actress."

"But you know the lines."

"Just because I read the script doesn't mean I memorized the lines," Barbara stressed, trying to pull her arm out her sister's grasp. "You're not going to get me to go out there and make a fool of myself."

Nikki's hopes plummeted as fast as they had risen.

"What about you?" Barbara suggested. "Nobody knows this script like you do."

"I'm not an actress," Nikki protested with the same horror her sister displayed just moments before.

"Yeah, but you seem to be a little short on those tonight," Barbara reminded her.

In sync, their watches beeped. A hush came over the whole theater.

"It's showtime," Barbara said, whispering the obvious.

Nikki felt ill, but she knew what she had to do. "Go out there and stall," she instructed Barbara. "I need two minutes. I'm going to have to go on."

"Are you sure?"

"You have a better idea?" she asked, in a voice that was ironically tinged with both sarcasm and hope.

Barbara gave Nikki a sympathetic smile, the kind you give when someone tells you that they only have twenty-four hours to live. "Okay. Break a leg, kid."

Nikki took off toward Crystal's dressing room—a janitor's closet—and quickly changed her clothes. As bad luck would have it, Crystal was a size smaller than Nikki and she was forced to cram her size eight hips into a size six dress.

It wasn't pretty.

She quickly tunneled her fingers through her hair to give it a very tousled and unkempt look, grabbed her antique hot comb prop, and then had to waddle like a penguin on crack back toward the stage. Standing stage left, Nikki took a deep breath and then waved frantically at her sister to let her know to wrap up her rambling speech.

Barbara brightened with relief. "And now…on with the show!"

There was a respectable applause as Barbara curtsied her way off the stage.

Nikki started praying and she kept on praying well after the house lights dimmed and the curtains parted.

The last thing in the world Hylan Dawson wanted to do was to go to a play—especially one entitled *Hot*

Comb & Hair Grease. This artsy-fartsy stuff was never his thing. Nevertheless, one of his New York playmates, Shonda, was calling herself an actress these days and she kept insisting on dragging him from one bad production to another. It was a high price to pay to get into her Victoria's Secrets, but a man had to do what a man had to do.

Shonda squeezed his hand as the house lights dimmed. "I'm so excited. My friend Crystal is the lead actress," she boasted in a low whisper. "I just know that you're going to love her."

Oh joy. Hylan smiled to camouflage his despair. If this Crystal chick's acting was as bad as Shonda's then he was truly in for a very long night. He turned his attention to the stage, drew a deep breath and prepared himself for anything.

Well, almost anything.

A woman waddled out on stage in a dress so tight he swore the entire front row could hear the seams screaming. Hylan didn't mind so much since the actress had an incredible body. She was stacked like a priceless work of art with full breasts, slim waist and rounded hips. If this play involved nudity it was definitely going to get two thumbs up and a couple of toes from him.

"That's *not* Crystal," Shonda hissed, frowning.

Good. That meant that Hylan could avoid a sticky situation between girlfriends when he slipped this black angel his number after the show. Sure the slick move would make him what women called a dog, but to him and his fellow Kappa Psi Kappa brothers it was what they considered exercising his options. Which for the record, he did on the regular. And why not? He was single, handsome and rich. Why shouldn't he shop around and play with all the toys his lifestyle afforded him?

Hylan smiled, wondering what her back view had to offer—something lush and squeezable he hoped. He took his time committing every curve of her incredible body to memory. When his gaze finally reached the actress's face, he sucked in a sudden breath at the sight of what could have only come straight out of his dreams. Her glowing oval face, plump full lips, crescent-shaped cheekbones and large doe-shaped eyes were a lethal combination to his heart...and his libido. Immediately, he started imagining how sexy she'd look draped in diamonds and writhing on a bed of black satin sheets.

Suddenly, his pants felt tight. He shifted in his chair and hoped that Shonda wouldn't notice.

"Isn't she going to say something?" Shonda whispered.

Hylan's brows jumped. Until that moment, he hadn't realized that while he was ogling the actress, she had been on the stage for at least a full two minutes and hadn't uttered a single word. In fact, she looked paralyzed—frightened.

Someone coughed in the audience, probably hoping that it would jar her out of her trance. When that didn't work, he could hear people shifting and grumbling. Still, his frozen angel stood in the center of the stage. A low murmur rippled around him. He watched as the woman's bottom lip trembled and her eyes watered. Clearly she was just seconds away from a breakdown.

He jumped to his feet.

"Where are you going?" Shonda hissed.

He blinked. Where *was* he going?

Finally a pencil-thin woman raced out on the stage and started whispering feverishly into the actress's ear. Whatever was said flicked on a switch and the actress quickly started babbling out dialogue at a clip that was mind-boggling and robotic as she waved a hot comb in the air.

Hylan lowered back into his chair. From Hylan's side, Shonda snickered. "She's awful."

Hylan agreed, but he was still fascinated by the beautiful actress. Who was this woman? How old was she? She looked young. Was she married? Had a man? If she had either of those things, was she happy? Shoot. A brother was just trying to get where he fit in.

The actress made a dramatic turn as other actors started to drift onto the stage, but when she did there was an audible rip. A gasp rose from the crowd as everyone was treated to a beautiful view of a pair of red-lace thong panties.

"Hot damn," Hylan mumbled under his breath as he gazed upon the most beautifully shaped ass he'd ever seen. Unfortunately, his exuberance was rewarded with a sharp elbow to the ribs and a narrowed glare from Shonda.

He tried to smooth it over with a lopsided smile that said, *Hey, I'm a man,* but Shonda just folded her arms until he melted back into his chair.

The initial shock gone, the audience roared with laughter.

The actress' face turned as red as her panties and she raced from the stage with tears streaking down her face.

The other actors stood stock-still for a few minutes and then continued even though the crowd was damn near in stitches and couldn't possibly hear what was being said on stage.

Hylan stood—ready to bolt backstage to check on the actress, but Shonda also stood and took his hand.

"C'mon," Shonda said. "This blows. Let's go back to your hotel…and play."

Hylan hesitated, an unusual reaction when a woman was offering up sex-on-a-platter. But he really wanted to check on that horrible actress and make sure that she was all right, and, of course, slip her his number—as long as she wasn't crying. He couldn't stand it when women cried.

"Hylan." Shonda tugged on his arm. "Let's go, baby."

What could he say? He had to leave with the one he came with. He smiled and then followed Shonda out of the row of seats. But as he, and a few others, shuffled up the aisle to the exit, he kept glancing back over his shoulder, wondering if the weeping actress would brave another appearance.

No such luck.

Chapter 2

To no one's great surprise, *Hot Comb & Hair Grease* opened and closed on the same night. For Nikki, reading the reviews was about as much fun as having her skin ripped from her body with a steel cat-o'-nine-tails. Nah. That would've been more fun.

Seriously.

For the next seven days, Nikki buried herself in her bed under a mile of sheets and comforters and kept the phone off the hook. She didn't watch television or listen to the radio. She just wanted silence, but was denied even that when a long line of concerned friends and family paraded up to her door and banged on it endlessly. Some even threatened to break it down, but then slumped away when Nikki called their bluff.

Even worse, in between visitors, Nikki couldn't shut

off her brain. All her woulda, shoulda, couldas just chased each other around her head until she was dizzy enough to pass out. When she woke the whole thing would just start all over again.

In the back of her mind, Nikki knew she was just being stubborn and childish. But she couldn't help it. Everything she'd dreamed of, worked for and slaved over had just blown up in her face. She was a joke in the theater world. Her name will become a verb. *You don't want to pull a Nikki Jamison on opening night.*

Nikki grabbed her favorite pillow and covered her head. "Aaarrrgh!" The scream felt good, but the relief it brought would only last for a couple of seconds. After that there would be more tears. More "what ifs," and "why me's".

And she still hadn't figured out what she was going to say to her parents. Somehow "sorry" didn't quite seem like it would be enough or even adequate. She just lost them a good chunk of their retirement money with no way of getting it back.

Her mother would just pretend like it didn't matter. Her father would demand that she face the truth and grow up—which she was willing to concede at this point and admit that maybe he was right. Maybe it was time for her to face the music—she was washed up. A has-been even before she'd ever been anything. Did that even make sense?

She had no problem imagining her parents' disappointed faces because it was a look she'd become accustomed to. Her mother would look like her smile was pinned on and her father would look as if he'd spent the last twenty years sucking on lemons.

Ella Joyce Jamison was a soft spoken woman—unless you started messing with her children—then she would turn into a raging lion. She was convinced that Nikki just wasn't challenged enough in life and tended to have an active imagination. This was all true. But Wilbur Jamison saw his daughter's inability to finish what she started as a sign of complete laziness and lack of discipline. There was a little bit of truth in that statement as well. At least it was true when it came to her dropping out of ballet, gymnastics, track, the softball team, the basketball team, college, design school and even cosmetology school. Every new hobby or project or school, her parents were right there—one reluctantly so—writing a check and hoping for the best.

The other parent rolled his eyes and counted the minutes until he could shout from the rooftops, "I told you so!"

This time, however, was different. Nikki did complete something. She wrote this damn play, financed it—well, begged her parents for the money—and even had an opening night. In some cynical way her father could read all of this as progress.

Then again, maybe she shouldn't hold her breath on that one.

Nikki removed the pillow from her head and just stared at the ceiling until she started making a game out of discovering different shapes and patterns in the chipped paint. A rattling at the front door caught her attention. Then there was the unmistakable sound of a key slipping into the lock.

Barbara.

She was the only person entrusted with a key to the studio apartment. Nikki closed her eyes and made a weak prayer for her baby sister to go away.

Nikki was the older sister. She was supposed to be the leader, grounded—someone her sister should or could look up to. Instead, Barbara was the perfect child. The child that could dance circles around Baryshnikov and play piano like she was born with keys glued to her fingertips. She was the straight-A student who was always at the top of every honor roll throughout her junior and high school years. From there she conquered medical school and was now dating a freaking neurosurgeon.

Bottom line: Barbara Rihanna Jamison was the daughter her father was *always* proud of—the one that he could never stop talking about. The one he kept saying Nikki needed to be more like.

"Nikki?" Barbara chirped when she cracked open the front door.

Nikki's hand shot out, grabbed the pillow again and smacked it down onto her head. She gave a less than one percent chance of her sister believing that she wasn't buried under the covers in the bed.

"Nikki?" Barbara rushed into the apartment, closed the door and then tiptoed her way toward the bedroom sectioned off by a room divider. When she reached the foot of her sister's bed, she started pulling the sheets and comforters from her sister's body. "I know you're in there, Nikki."

"Go away!" Nikki shouted into the pillow.

"I can't." Barbara said. "Not until I at least know that you're okay."

The pillow popped off again. "See. I'm okay." She forced a joker's smile. "Now go away!"

The ever-smiling Barbara cocked her head. "You can't lie in bed all day."

"Sure I can. Watch me." Nikki rolled over and tried to pull the comforter back over her body, but Barbara held a firm grip and refused to let go. Instead of giving up, Nikki redoubled her efforts and before she knew it, she was engaged in a full fledged tug-of-war.

"Let go," Nikki hissed, tugging.

"You're acting ridiculous," Barbara reasoned, tugging right back.

"So what! Nobody asked you to come here anyway." *Tug.*

"I was worried!" *Tug.*

"Well, who asked you to worry? I just want to be left alone!" *Tug.*

"Fine!" Barbara let go of the comforter just when Nikki was about to throw her full weight on the next tug.

Next thing Nikki knew she was careening over the side of the bed and the left side of her face smacking against the hardwood floor. "Ow."

"Ohmigod, Nikki!" Barbara raced around the bed. "Are you all right?" She knelt down and turned her sister over onto her side. "It sounded like you hit your head." She immediately started examining her.

"Will you stop it?" Nikki said, pulling away.

"Just hold still. I need to make sure that you don't have a concussion."

Nikki swatted her sister's hands away. "I'm fine."

Barbara finally snapped. "Why are you always fighting me?"

"Why do always think you can fix things?" Nikki barked as her eyes welled with tears. "You can't fix this, Barbara. So please, *please* stop trying."

Her little sister's eyes glossed with tears as her bottom lip started trembling. "Okay." She glanced around. "Then I guess I better…" She stood up and hand-ironed her skirt down. "I'll just…talk to you later." Barbara turned and headed toward the door.

Nikki watched as her sister walked away with her shoulders slumped and her head hung low and felt like a complete ass for blowing up at her. "Barb," she called.

But Barbara didn't stop walking.

"Barbara!"

Her sister opened the front door and then slammed it behind her.

Fearing that she had finally done it, Nikki jumped to her feet and ran after her. "Barbara!" *Damn, me and my big mouth.* She gave chase all the way out of the building, but like in everything else, Barbara was a better runner, too. *Great. Just great.*

Later that night, Nikki's girlfriends Antoinette and Gwen pulled off a miracle and actually managed to get

Nikki out of her self-imposed exile and dragged her down to their favorite hole-in-the-wall club, Sparkle. The place was fairly popular with the artsy crowd where everyone pretty much just bragged about whatever project they managed to snag over the loud eighties music.

"See. Don't you feel better getting out of the house?" Antoinette said, wearing her usual sunny smile.

As far as Nikki knew there wasn't a tragedy that Antoinette couldn't put a positive spin on. That habit had a way of being both endearing and annoying. "I guess it's all right."

"Well, I think it's awfully brave of you," Gwen said, expressing her usually pessimistic view. "Had it been me up there flashing my ass to a theater full of people, I wouldn't come out of my apartment for at least a couple of years."

"Good night," Nikki turned around on her bar stool and started to climb off when Antoinette grabbed her by the shoulders.

"No. You're not going anywhere." She twirled Nikki back around. "Gwen, you're not helping."

Gwen shrugged her shoulders. "I'm just keepin' it real."

"No. You're just—"

"Just let it go," Nikki said. "I'm not in the mood to play referee." She held up her empty glass toward the female bartender that was splitting her time between flirting with the male customers and working. "Refill."

"Isn't that your third drink?" Antoinette asked.

"Oh, please," Gwen rolled her eyes. "The only time to get concerned is when she starts ordering drinks that actually have alcohol in them."

Nikki twisted her face into a comical frown. "I may be depressed, but I still know that me and alcohol don't mix."

"Amen," Antoinette agreed. No doubt she was remembering a college spring break that landed Nikki a starring role in *Girls Gone Wild*.

"Another *virgin* piña colada?" the bartender asked in a dull voice.

"If you don't mind." Nikki smiled tightly because she detected the woman was struggling to refrain from rolling her eyes.

"Comin' right up." She took Nikki's empty glass and walked away.

Once her back was turned, Nikki felt free to roll her eyes first. Then as she started to turn her attention back to her two girlfriends, she caught a few stares and hand-pointing aimed in her direction. "Just great," she mumbled under her breath.

"Don't pay them any mind," Antoinette said, without having to be told what Nikki was referring to—which meant that she saw them, too.

"Yeah," Gwen said and then yelled above the music. "What the hell are y'all looking at?"

The staring and pointing stopped. Not too many people were bold enough to challenge Gwen. On top of being loud and boisterous, she was a very large and rather intimidating woman who'd rather knuckle up than talk it out.

"Mmm-hmm. That's what I thought," Gwen mumbled.

Nikki shook her head. She didn't know if her friend was making it better or worse.

"One virgin piña colada," the bartender said, returning. "I even added an extra pineapple wedge."

"Thanks," Nikki deadpanned. But as she stared down at the tropical drink, she didn't really have the urge to drink it. "Maybe Gwen is right," she said. "It's too soon for all of this."

Gwen bobbed her head in agreement.

"Nonsense. Whenever you fall off a horse, you get back up," Antoinette said, pushing Nikki's drink toward her.

Nikki didn't respond. She was too busy listening to Michael Jackson scream "Beat It."

"Maybe what you need is a little vacation," Antoinette finally conceded, "someplace where you can just get away from the hustle and bustle of the city."

"Yeah, someplace where they don't know your name," Gwen added.

Antoinette angled a hard glare at her friend.

"What? I'm just keepin' it real."

"Well, unless this magical place can be reached by the subway, I can't afford it. And hell, to be honest, I can't afford that."

Her friends' faces collapsed in disappointment. After a few jams from Bobby Brown and Prince, Nikki sighed. "It would be nice to get away." She took a long sip of her frosty drink. "Somewhere tropical, exotic."

"Hmm. I know a place like that," said a woman sitting to Nikki's right.

"Really?"

The woman shrugged. "I used to date this really good-looking guy out in Atlanta. Actually, he was more along the lines of *gorgeous*." She laughed. "Anyway, he has a beautiful vacation home out in Saint Lucia that he hardly ever goes to. Have you ever been to Saint Lucia?"

Nikki shook her head.

"Beautiful." The woman rolled her eyes. "White sand and a breathtakingly blue ocean. And the people there are so nice. There's not a day that I don't dream about going back to that island. Hell, I could stay at that big old empty house of his and he'd never know it." She laughed.

Nikki perked up. "Really?"

"Really," the woman reaffirmed.

The wheels in Nikki's head started turning and a smile started to creep across her face.

"Oh, how I wish I could have snagged a ring from that man."

"Why didn't you?" Gwen asked, leaning forward. It was nothing for Gwen to jump into someone else's Kool-Aid and stir it around.

"Because Hylan Dawson is *not* the marrying kind."

Chapter 3

18 months later...

Gisella's and Charlie Masters's hands overlapped as they gripped the knife and together sliced into a popular Sinful Chocolate creation: white chocolate and lemon cake. The happy couple smiled at the wedding photographer and then at each other before shoving a handful of the decadent dessert into each other's faces.

Laughter rippled through the large gathering of friends and family and then a cheer went up when Charlie then tried to kiss and lick his wife's face clean.

"I love you, baby," he whispered, snapping their

bodies together despite the small baby bump and dipping his head for a long, soulful kiss. She tasted so sweet.

"Je t'aime aussi," she responded when he allowed her to come up for air.

Charlie groaned at the instant hard-on he acquired whenever Gisella spoke French. Now that they've said their I dos, Charlie was ready to skip right to the honeymoon, so much so he found himself asking Gisella every five minutes, "Can we leave now?"

Charlie laughed as his mother gripped his cheeks and tried to pinch the blood out of them. "My baby has made me so proud. Not only did you give me a beautiful daughter-in-law, but I'm finally getting my grandbaby."

"Anything for you, Mama." He kissed her cheek.

"Of course you know I was right," she added, releasing his cheeks. "Didn't I tell you if you found a woman who could cook like your mama then you had a winner?"

"That you did, Mama." He wrapped his arm around her.

"I just wish your father was here to see this day," she said. "Married and about to become a father. He would be so proud. I am."

"Thanks Mom." He kissed her lovingly on her upturned cheek.

"Mama Arlene," Taariq Bryson, a fellow Kappa Psi Kappa brother, greeted her with a wide smile. "I don't know if Charlie told you, but we talked it over and he's completely cool with calling me Daddy. All you have to do now is accept my proposal. I'll make an honest woman out of you."

"You're so bad." Arlene blushed as she gave Taariq a welcoming hug. "Now when are *you* getting married?"

"As soon as you say yes."

She rolled her eyes. "You just love me for my fried chicken."

"That's not true. You make a mean sweet potato pie, too."

Arlene laughed and then continued to giggle like a schoolgirl when Taariq asked for a dance. As he led her to the dance floor, Charlie was left to shake his head.

"So you finally did it," Hylan said, stepping forward and slapping his large hand across Charlie's back. "You waved the white flag and surrendered to the enemy."

Charlie laughed and rolled his eyes. "Don't start that with me."

"What?" He hunched his shoulders. "I'm just saying. We were supposed to be playas for life. Remember?"

Derrick Knight, another fraternity brother, rushed up behind Hylan and quickly put him in a headlock. "Whatever he's saying, don't listen to him."

"Oh, he's harmless." Charlie chuckled. "I'm just waiting for the day when he starts waving his own white flag."

"It'll never happen," Hylan croaked from under Derrick's arm.

"It doesn't make any sense to be so hardheaded," Derrick said, releasing him.

Hylan inhaled a deep breath and then playfully

lunged a left jab at Derrick's shoulder. "Mark my words. A brother like me ain't going down without a fight. You'll have to pry my playa card out of my cold dead hands."

"All right," Derrick said. "We're going to hold you to that."

"Charlie," said Stanley, the only white Kappa brother in their clique, as he joined the group. "Your wife's cake is off the hook. What's her secret, man?"

"She didn't make this cake. Her assistant Pamela insisted on making the cake as a gift. She did a good job."

"Pamela, huh? Where is she?" Stanley turned to survey the crowd. "Maybe I'll marry her."

"I'm sure she'll be thrilled to hear it," Charlie laughed. "Start with baby steps. Try to get a date first."

"Or try to get a woman to stand still long enough for you to introduce yourself," Hylan added, laughing. It was a tradition to give the lanky redhead a hard time.

"Ha-ha. Ya'll gonna get enough messing with me." Stanley scanned the crowd again. "There's gotta be someone here I can hook up with. Weddings are the best places for single people to hook up. That and funerals."

Hylan and Charlie just stared at him.

"What? It's what I heard."

"We're going to pray for you," Hylan said, rolling his eyes. How Stanley managed to hang with them for fifteen years and still be as square as he was was something short of amazing.

"Whatever." Stanley moved his lanky frame closer

to Charlie. "So now that you're off the market, what do you say to passing a playa like me your infamous little black book? I've heard that it's a pretty thick book."

"A playa like you?" Hylan snickered. "If anyone should inherit the Holy Grail from my man here, it should be me."

"Guys, guys. As much as I'd like to improve your game, I can't. Gisella and I had a nice farewell ceremony and then tossed the book into the fireplace."

Hylan and Stanley blinked and then both pointed at him accusingly. "Judas!"

Derrick and Charlie laughed.

"What do a couple of married women have to do to get a dance with their husbands?"

Derrick and Charlie turned toward their smiling wives.

"Not a thing," Charlie said, taking his wife into his arms. "Of course I'm looking forward to a little private dance," he whispered as he led her toward the music.

"Oh you'll get your dance, Mr. Masters. That and a whole lot more."

"That's what I'm counting on, Mrs. Masters. That's what I'm counting on."

Still smiling, Hylan shook his head. Two of the five Kappa brothers were down for the count. He still couldn't believe it. Hell, it seems like it was just yesterday when they were all piled into Herman's Barbershop and giving each other dabs and swearing that a honey would never lock them down. "Playas for life," they had all vowed.

Now look at them.

Hylan, along with most of the wedding guests,

watched the bride and groom glide across the floor to an old Luther Vandross classic. He had to admit that his buddy, Charlie, had certainly snagged himself a beautiful woman. Gisella glowed like an angel as she stared up into her husband's eyes and Charlie looked… happy. In fact, Hylan had never seen him so happy.

There was a sudden tightening in Hylan's chest. His throat constricted and his eyes…

A waiter waltzed by and Hylan snatched a flute of champagne from his tray and downed the contents in one long gulp while he tried to shake off whatever the heck that feeling was coming over him. "Maybe it's just heartburn," he mumbled as he set the now-empty flute on the next tray that passed by.

"Need an antacid?" Stanley asked, popping out of nowhere and grinning like one of those funny-looking orange Cheshire cats.

Hylan jumped and cocked an arm back. "Man, you're going to get tired of sneaking up on me like that."

Stanley laughed. "Don't blame me. You ought to stop being so damn scary."

"Ha-ha." Hylan rolled his eyes.

"So where's your girl at?"

That was a good question. Hylan's gaze scanned the perimeter a couple of times and came up empty. "Why is it when women go to the bathroom, they stay in there forever?" he asked.

"Like I would know." Stanley jammed his hands deep into his pants pockets and rocked on his heels. "So what's the 4-1-1 with you and Shonda? Y'all together again?"

Hylan shrugged. "We're just kickin' it. Why?"

Stanley smirked. "Just asking."

Hylan stretched the collar of his dress shirt and then grabbed another flute of champagne from yet another tray. "It's *not* what you're thinking."

"Of course not."

After busting out some old school moves with Charlie's mother, Taariq bowed to the older woman and then made his way over to his two best friends. "Well, it looks like another one bites the dust, fellas. I still can't believe it." He swung his gaze over to Hylan. "I gotta tell ya. I thought you'd fall before old Charlie."

Hylan choked on the rest of his champagne. "Who, me?"

Taariq swatted him on the back. "You all right?"

Once Hylan finally managed to suck enough air into his lungs, he waved Taariq off. "How the hell can you say something like that? It's like you're calling me outta my Christian name or something."

"All right. Don't be overly dramatic," Taariq said, shrugging. "It's just that…you know…you and Shonda hooked up again."

"And? Just because I'm seeing some chick I used to date a while back you think that's just cause for me to jump off a cliff?"

"I've just never known you to recycle."

Hylan cut his gaze toward Stanley.

"Me, either," Stanley said.

"*And* you brought her to the wedding," Taariq added.

"So? It's just a pit stop. We're flying out to Saint

Lucia this afternoon for a little sun and fun. I haven't had a vacation in I don't know how long—and I need one." Which was the truth. Dawson Engineering was still doing well, even in a down economy and was on pace to becoming Atlanta's largest and most innovative technology provider. Hylan was in an industry where being a workaholic was required.

But the times he carved out to play—he played hard.

Taariq laughed and snapped his fingers in front of Hylan's face. "C'mon, man. This is basic Playa Handbook 101 stuff here. You never bring a chick to a wedding unless you plan on marrying her. You bring a chick here and they get to seeing a wedding dress and all these pretty flower arrangements, and the next thing you know they're plotting how they're going to get *you* down the aisle.

Hylan started bobbing his head. Taariq was right. What the heck was he thinking? He liked Shonda. They always had a good time together—but making her wifey or wife was definitely not in the cards.

Just then Hylan caught sight of Shonda threading her way through the crowd. The young, budding actress drew her fair share of stares, but it probably had more to do with the fact she was wearing an outfit better suited for a hooker—an extremely short silk mini-dress that left nothing to the imagination.

The men in attendance seemed to like it.

The women…not so much.

Hylan glanced at his watch. "It's about that time. I'm

outta here." He turned and gave both Stanley and Taariq half hugs and fist bumps.

"What? You're not going to wait for the garter toss?" Taariq teased.

"Get the hell out of here with that mess, man." Hylan laughed and then strolled across the pavilion to retrieve his date.

Shonda didn't see Hylan and was still scanning the crowd and bouncing anxiously on her toes when he eased up behind her and wrapped his arm around her small waist. "Looking for me?"

Shonda jumped and gasped, but as soon as she realized who it was, she relaxed and turned in his arms to face him. "I've got great news," she beamed.

Her excitement was so contagious, Hylan's smile stretched equally as wide. "All right. Lay it on me."

"I just received a call from Nick Jones. *The* Nick Jones," she said squealing. "He wants me in his latest movie. Can you believe it?"

Actually, he couldn't. "Well, that's great. It looks like it'll be a vacation slash celebration in Saint Lucia this week." He glanced at his watch again. "Are you about ready to go?"

"Oh, I can't go," she said, eyes blinking. "Nick wants me out in L.A. tomorrow."

"What?"

Shonda looped her arms around Hylan's neck and pressed her large breasts against his chest while she poked her lips out into a fake pout. "You understand, don't you? It's *the* Nick Jones."

Hylan's spirits plummeted with disappointment, but he hid it with a perfect mask of understanding. "Sure. I understand."

Looks like I'm flying solo on this vacation.

Chapter 4

Hylan loved Saint Lucia.

The minute the plane touched down, he could feel the stress of his job roll off of him in waves. How could it not? Everywhere he looked was a postcard-perfect snapshot—despite the gathering clouds. The Atlantic Ocean kissed the northern shores of the small island while the Caribbean Sea hugged the west coast. The twin coastal peaks soared two-thousand feet from the sea and were blanketed with an emerald-colored rain forest.

From the moment the private jet touched down in the Soufrière quarter, Hylan shut off his BlackBerry and mentally checked out for vacation. Stepping off the plane, he swore that the air smelled fresher, the sun was brighter and life just plain sweeter. "Why don't I come here more often?" he said under his breath. The answer was truly a mystery. Whenever he was rushing around making deals, he repeatedly told himself that he didn't have time for a vacation. And whenever he did make time, he always wondered why he didn't do it more often.

Hylan's maternal roots ran deep on the island. When he was a child, he remembered spending long summer days diving, snorkeling, sailing, windsurfing, hiking— you name it, he did it. His parents never had a lot of money, but everyone who knew Hylan Sr. and Sabelle Dawson knew that they were rich with love. Hylan had been their miracle child, having been conceived when his mother was in her late forties after nearly two decades of hoping and praying.

As a result, Hylan may have been a little spoiled.

A horn blared.

Hylan looked up to see a green Jeep speeding toward him near the small hangar. The man was going so fast, Hylan wondered if he needed to dive out of the way before being hit. At the last minute, the driver slammed on the brakes and stopped within inches of him.

"Bonjour, Mr. Dawson," the islander shouted a half a second before he jumped out of the vehicle and swept Hylan into a full-body hug. "Welcome home!"

Hylan's face contorted in confusion, but he managed to put on something that resembled a smile by the time the man released him. "Gotta tell you, me and the missus were starting to wonder if you were ever coming back. Nikki kept insisting that you were coming and… well…here you are!"

"Here I am," Hylan said. *Who in the hell is this guy?* Knowing how small the island was, chances were that he was probably embracing some cousin or family member.

"It was just by chance that I was out here dropping off a couple of tourists who were staying at the Anse Chastanet resort when someone said that you were on this flight. You picked a helluva time to arrive with a storm brewing."

Hylan glanced up. It never ceased to amaze him just how quickly storm clouds gathered over the island.

"Do you need a ride to the house?" the man asked.

"Actually, I was just going to call for—"

"Forget it. I'll take you. Where're your bags?" He glanced around just as a young teenager appeared, struggling with Hylan's luggage.

The driver let out a loud whistle and then yelled a long stream of Antillean Creole at the teen. "I guess it's a good thing that I came along when I did. Does Nikki know you were coming today?"

"I—"

"Of course she does. What the hell am I thinking?" He laughed and showed his entire top and bottom row of teeth.

Hylan felt as if he was supposed to join in, so he did. "You know, you really don't have to—"

"Nonsense. I got to go out and see Momma Mahina anyway."

"Mahina," Hylan said, happy to finally recognize the name of his housekeeper in the confusing torrent of words the man hurled at him. "You're Mahina's son?"

"Nephew, but she's like a second mom *so* I call her Momma." The driver chuckled and then smacked his head. "Where are my manners?" He thrust out his hand. "The name is Rafiq. Momma Mahina and Nikki talk about you so much I feel as though I already know you."

Hylan's laugh turned genuine as he finally started to relax around the chatty driver. "Well, in that case, if you're going my way, I'd love to hitch a ride."

"Good." Rafiq's bright smile was as white as his skin was black. "As you Americans say, let's get this show on the road." His large hand smacked across Hylan's back before he turned and snapped at the teenager to hurry up. "Mr. Dawson doesn't have all day, son."

"Mr. Dawson?" The tall, lanky teenager's eyes perked up with curiosity as he pulled his thick dreads back from his eyes. If Hylan didn't know any better, he would have sworn that he detected a hint of hostility from the teen. *What the hell is this kid's problem?*

The still chuckling Rafiq leaned in with a loud whisper, "Don't pay Adal any mind. Everyone thinks he has the hots for Nikki. Then again, I'd say Nikki has cast most men in the quarter under her spell." He winked and elbowed Hylan in his side. "Teenagers. The boy is harmless."

Adal scowled at Rafiq for ratting him out about his crush on this Nikki chick. Hylan tried to smooth things over by giving the young man a generous tip after he dumped his luggage in the back of the Jeep, but Adal just looked at Hylan's gratuity as if he'd shoved a snake at him, and then stormed off.

Rafiq's head rocked back with a hearty gust of laughter. "Aw yeah. The boy got it bad."

"Oookay." Hylan crammed the money back into his pants pocket and then climbed into the passenger side of the Jeep.

Rafiq was still laughing when he slammed his foot down on the accelerator of the lightweight four-wheeler and sped away from the airport hangar.

Almost immediately, Hylan grabbed the side door, half way expecting the G-force speed to rip him right out of his seat.

"Now that you're back, I'm sure the local gossip will finally die down. I don't mind telling you that people in the quarter was split down the middle as to whether you were ever going to come back." He grinned over at Hylan. "I have to admit, I had my doubts, too. But then again Nikki is a *very* beautiful woman. The kind men usually just put on a shelf."

Hylan frowned. *What the hell is this dude talking about?*

Rafiq temporarily took his hands off the steering wheel in mock surrender. "I don't mean no disrespect, man. It's none of my business. It's just an observation, if you know what I mean."

"Not really." The Jeep swerved out of its lane and Hylan caught sight of a speeding truck, heading toward them. His heart leapt into his throat as he reached over for the wheel. "Pay attention to the road!"

Rafiq nonchalantly took control of the wheel. "No problem, man. I got this."

Hylan glared as he eased back to his side of the

vehicle. He didn't travel all the way back to paradise so that he could become someone's hood ornament.

"It's just that, in the past, I've known you to come here with different women," Rafiq continued as if their lives hadn't just been snatched out of the jaws of death. "All of them beautiful," he added hastily. "But in my opinion none of them comes close to Nikki. She's beautiful both inside and out. Everyone in the quarter will testify to that. She's been involved with everything from the Dunnottar School for children with disabilities to the Holy Family Charity Home. I swear sometimes if you look closely enough, you can actually see her wings. She's beautiful, smart, kind, generous and…" he stabbed Hylan with a sharp look "…patient. Truly an angel."

Is he trying to fix me up with this chick? "I see," Hylan said. He had to admit that his interest was piqued a little bit. What was there not to like about a beautiful woman who was also smart? "And where is Nikki now?"

Rafiq shrugged. "I imagine at the house. She's told everyone that she's working on a new script. After having writer's block for so long, this is good news, no?"

"At the house?" Hylan struggled to keep up with the conversation.

"Oh wait 'til you see. Nikki has done an amazing job redecorating the place. Not to mention she's been a godsend for Momma Mahina. You know she will never admit that she's getting on in years and can't do the things she used to do."

Hylan felt as if he'd finally put the pieces to this strange puzzle together. Mahina hired an assistant that had apparently become the talk of the quarter. "So Nikki works with Mahina?"

"And thank the good Lord. After Hurricane Richard blew through here nine months ago, Momma Mahina needed all the help she could get."

Hylan nodded, remembering hearing about the storm. His assistant had kept him abreast of all the repairs with his insurance company, his accountant, and his property manager, Mahina. With his company growing and the demands on his time, Hylan had put his complete trust in Mahina's abilities and it sounded as if it had paid off. "Well, I'll make sure that I thank Nikki personally for helping hold down the fort."

"I bet you will." Rafiq winked and then reached over and turned up the radio. The unmistakable voice of Saint Lucia native Taj Weekes boomed loudly from the speakers. Hylan and Rafiq bobbed their heads in time to the melodic bass. The music was the perfect backdrop to the lush, verdant scenery of wild orchids, giant ferns and Caribbean flamingos. And Soufrière was different from the other Saint Lucia quarters because it had the world's only drive-in volcanic crater. Hylan always made a point of visiting it whenever he was on the island and could already feel himself getting excited at the prospect of seeing the sulfur springs again.

As the music of Weekes faded out, Rafiq turned the radio back down and grinned at Hylan. "So are you staying long or are you just swooping in to take our lovely Nikki away from us?"

"I'm just in for two weeks." Hylan struggled to keep his grin from turning cocky. Rafiq seemed extremely confident in Hylan's game when it came to women. But if this Nikki chick was even half the dime-piece Rafiq thought she was, then Hylan would be down for whatever. Vacations were always best when they were spent with the opposite sex. "But I can be persuaded to stay longer."

Rafiq's cocky grin matched Hylan's as he made a sharp left on a rustic coastal road that ascended to Dawson's private estate. Once they cleared the overgrown foliage, the two-story white, palatial villa stretched up toward a darkening blue sky.

"Looks like we're in for a rough one," Hylan observed.

"What are you going to do? It's that time of year." Rafiq said as he slammed on the brakes.

Hylan's hands shifted from the door to the dashboard, which he was certain he was just seconds from sailing through. Before he could curse the driver out, Rafiq had jumped from behind the wheel and started unloading the bags.

"Welcome home," Rafiq declared and then marched up toward the front door.

Hylan stumbled out of the vehicle on shaky legs and grabbed the two remaining bags. The moment he crossed the threshold however, he pulled up short and wondered if Rafiq had taken him to the right house. "What the…"

"Looks good, doesn't it?" Rafiq said, bobbing

his head and smiling as if he expected Hylan to turn cartwheels or something.

He almost did. Not that he didn't like his house before with its pristine, airy, white décor that, quite frankly, most villas—whether they were homes or resorts—showcased. His spacious vacation villa now looked both modern and urbane, intimate, masculine, quiet and sophisticated—especially with its coffee-colored walls.

"This looks like it cost me a fortune," he said. His gaze danced across the room with its new furniture and an array of eclectic artworks.

Rafiq shrugged. "I don't know about such things. You'd have to ask the missus about that."

Hylan bobbed his head, but then when Rafiq's words registered, he frowned and turned his head toward him. "Ask who?"

"All I'm saying is that a man's house is his castle, no?"

Hylan started to answer when this angelic voice floated down from the second level. "Rafiq, is that you?"

Hylan didn't think it was possible but the man's smile stretched even wider as he brushed a hand over his bushy, uneven 'fro.

"Yes, ma'am."

The woman laughed and it sounded like sweet music to Hylan's ears.

"I thought so. I'd recognize that engine anywhere. When are you going to get a tune-up?"

Obviously embarrassed, Rafiq's broad smile dimmed

as he kicked the tiled floor in the foyer. "Soon. I'll get it to the shop later this week. Promise."

"Yeah. Yeah. Can you go help Momma Mahina out in the guesthouse? We're storm-proofing all the windows."

"Yes, ma'am." Rafiq started bowing even though the woman had yet to grace him with her presence. "By the way Nikki, I, um, brought you home a gift." He poked another sharp elbow into Hylan's ribs.

Hylan flinched, but not before debating whether to send a quick jab upside Rafiq's head. He spared him this time, but if the man elbowed him again, all bets were off.

"No more gifts, Rafiq," the woman said, her voice becoming clearer as she approached the top of the stairs. "I told you that I'm a happily married woman." She stepped into view and froze.

Hylan's eyes widened with a sudden jolt of recognition—like any man could ever forget those stacked curves or even that face. "You." In the next second, he felt as if he was spiraling out of control in some mad man's vertigo. He dropped the bags that were in his hands and at the last second managed a little more strength in his knees. Was he dreaming or was he seeing that New York actress's twin? They say everyone has one.

After a few more seconds, Hylan felt as if he was getting his bearings back—at least that's what he took his growing hard-on to mean.

"Ah, Nikki, I knew you'd like this gift," Rafiq

boasted, slamming his large, bony hand against the center of Hylan's back.

Nikki? This was the infamous woman Rafiq bragged about? Hylan dropped his gaze so that he could take in the pleasure of its slow climb back up her body. This certainly had the makings of becoming a memorable vacation.

Rafiq's laughter bubbled between the silent couple. "Looks like I was wrong. Nikki didn't know you were coming. You old dog." He delivered another whack against Hylan's back, before he then leaned over and whispered, "About that gift thing, that's just a little inside joke between us two. I would never hit on your wife."

Rafiq's declaration may as well have been a sucker punch. *"My wife!"*

Chapter 5

Oh shit.

That was the only thing that kept looping around inside Nikki's head. No, she didn't personally know the man standing at the bottom of the stairs. But she knew from the fair amount of pictures she'd seen in the house and from his many legions of cousins on the island that he was in fact the man she had been masquerading as being married to for the past year and a half. With nosy Rafiq looking on, she knew that she had to do something—preferably before her *husband* exposed her for the fraud that she was.

"Honey, you're home." She forced a smile across her face and then willed her legs to run down the stairs. "Why didn't you call and tell me that you were coming?" As she hit the bottom stair, she opened her arms and then launched herself toward the complete stranger.

Inwardly, Nikki tried to prepare herself for the man to ward off her exuberant greeting, but instead he allowed her to wrap her arms around him and plant her lips against his. She meant for it to be just a small peck, but the minute their mouths connected, something unexpected charged through her—something nice, warm and downright magical.

The moan wasn't part of the impromptu performance, but Hylan's response was to fold his arms around her slim waist and pick her up a full four inches off the ground. It was either the sudden airlift or his incredible mouth that had her head reeling—she couldn't decide which.

Damn. He can kiss.

Another pair of feet shuffled toward the foyer a second before Momma Mahina's unmistakable husky voice boomed, "Nikki, chile. The windows out at the guesthouse have all been taken care of and…Oh, my Lord! Is that who I think it is?"

Hylan's and Nikki's lips broke apart. Their eyes locked and reflected the same level of shock. Clearly whatever she was feeling, he felt it, too.

"It is!" Momma Mahina clapped her hands together and let out a loud shriek and she raced over to Hylan, her large bottom swaying back and forth until she reached her longtime employer and enveloped both him and his wife in her arms. "I can't believe it. You're finally home."

It's been a year and a half and Nikki still hadn't

grown used to Momma Mahina's hugs. The sweet woman could choke a boa constrictor to death before she realized that she needed to let go.

"You want to ease up on that death grip, Mahina?" Hylan croaked.

Momma Mahina's arms sprang open and Nikki quickly sucked in a few gulps of air despite her aching rib cage.

However, Mahina's excitement quickly changed and she delivered a quick slap to Hylan's arm. "How dare you stay away for so long!" She smacked him again and then jerked Nikki out of his arms to pull her against her heavy bosom. "I can't believe that you've been so heartless as to leave this poor chile here all alone. If I was her I would have left you a long time ago!"

Hylan's brows jumped up as he lazily folded his arms in front of his chest. "Is that right?"

Nikki shut her eyes as if that would somehow make her invisible.

"You have a good woman here," Mahina said. "Don't forget that I knew your mother and I know for a fact that she would *not* have been pleased about the way you've been treating her." She waved her finger at Hylan as if she'd just caught him stealing. "I know that you think that becoming some big shot businessman is important, but let me tell you that all the money in the world is never gonna bring you even half the happiness that a good woman can."

Somebody shoot me now, Nikki prayed.

After a long silence, Hylan said, "You're right."

Nikki peeled one eye open. *Did I just hear what I think I heard?*

Hylan's dark gaze shifted from Momma Mahina to Nikki. "I've been a fool for staying away for so long. One thing I plan on doing is make up for this long absence to...*my wife.*" His lips twitched. "That's if she'll let me."

He's not going to expose me. Nikki's knees threatened to give way in relief.

Momma Mahina's baritone laugh rumbled through her chest and shook her entire body. "See. Now *that's* the sweet boy I remember." She released Nikki to move in closer and gather Hylan's cheeks in her fingers, and then gave them a good, hard pinch. "I'm glad to hear that you've finally come back to your senses. I swear that if I ever hear of you mistreating this good girl, I won't hesitate to turn you over my knee."

Hylan laughed and tried to pull away from her grip before her fingerprints were permanently indented on his face.

"Don't laugh," Rafiq said. "She's dead serious."

"Better listen to the boy," Momma Mahina said, releasing his face. "I turned his grown butt over my lap just last week for breaking my great nana's china. Didn't I, Rafiq?"

"The woman's hand must have weighed about fifty pounds," Rafiq deadpanned.

"In that case, I'll considered myself warned." Hylan reached out and pulled Nikki back to his side.

Why am I melting in his arms?

What she needed to do was think of exactly how

she was going to explain to a stranger just why it was she'd been masquerading as his wife. Unfortunately, it seemed her creative mind had hit another writer's block because she was coming up with zilch.

"In that case," Momma Mahina said, walking past them to grab her jacket, "I'll leave you two to your happy reunion. Who knows, maybe we'll have an addition to the family nine months from now, eh?" She slapped him on the arm and Rafiq followed with another sharp elbow.

What the hell? Am I in the middle of a WWE match and don't know it? He glanced over at *his wife* and concluded that at this point anything was possible.

When it was clear that the two were getting ready to leave, Nikki suddenly bolted out of Hylan's arms. "Wait!"

Momma Mahina jumped at the sudden shout. "What? What is it, chile?"

"You can't leave," Nikki said.

"Why not?"

Nikki bumped her lips together but no words came.

"Yes, *sweetheart*. Why can't they leave?" Hylan asked, rubbing his arm.

Nikki didn't know the man and couldn't discern whether he was irritated or amused. Lord knows she was hoping it was the latter. The last thing she wanted to do tonight was go to jail. Realizing that everyone was waiting for her to say something, she forced words to spill out of her mouth and just prayed that it would make sense.

"Storm. Coming. We…um, should probably just all hunker down here…together…*all* of us."

One side of Hylan's lips twitched again.

Momma Mahina clucked her tongue and rolled her eyes. "See what I mean?" she asked Hylan. "Such a sweet chile. Always worried about others." She returned her attention to Nikki, this time grabbing her cheeks and giving them a healthy pinch. "Rafiq and I will be fine. We've survived many a storm. Besides, I have to make sure Lathan's dinner is on the table by six. He gets very grouchy when it's late—storm or no storm."

"Then I should come help you," Nikki insisted.

Momma Mahina and Rafiq frowned.

"What the heck is wrong with you, chile?" the older woman said, jabbing her fists against the curve of her waist. "You got your own man here that needs tending to." Her gaze darted between Hylan and Nikki with sudden suspicion.

Nikki teetered between panic and downright hysteria. Once again, Hylan surprised her by coming to her aide and wrapping his strong arms around her waist. "I couldn't agree with you more, Mahina. *My wife* and I have a lot of catching up to do." He glanced at Nikki. "Isn't that right, sweetie?" He leaned down and peppered her long neck with small kisses.

Nikki quivered and swallowed a soft moan.

Mahina's and Rafiq's faces exploded with smiles.

"Yes. You stay here and take care of your man." She reached out and patted Nikki directly on her flat belly. "Nothing like a new baby in the spring."

Nikki's mouth fell open.

Hylan reached over and gently pushed her chin up to close it. "We'll see you all later."

"Yes. I'll make sure to call before coming over," she joked, winking.

Before Nikki could think of any way to stop them, Mahina and Rafiq slipped out of the door. Hylan stood at the threshold for a few more seconds, waving them off.

Nikki eased from his side and started to tiptoe toward the staircase. That is until she heard the distinctive click of the door behind her.

"Going somewhere, *honey?*" Hylan asked.

Wincing, Nikki slowly made a one-hundred-eighty degree turn and hit Hylan with a *please don't hurt me* expression.

He crossed his arms and continued to look both amused and annoyed. "Forgive me, sweetheart, but, um…I don't exactly remember our wedding…or proposing. Hell, for that matter, even being properly introduced."

"Oh!" Nikki adjusted her 5'9" frame and thrust a hand out to him. "Nicole Dawson."

Hylan's brows jumped.

"Uh." Her hand fell down as she shook her head. "I meant, um, Nicole Jamison."

A hard vein popped up along Hylan's jawline while his mahogany eyes transformed into polished onyx.

No doubt about it. He's mad.

"I'm sure you're probably wondering why people seemed to think that we're married," she started, taking a tentative step backward.

Hylan stepped forward. "No. Actually, I think I have that part figured out."

"You do?" she asked, surprised.

"Yeah. You *lied* to them."

She tried to laugh but they both knew that there wasn't a damn thing funny about this situation. "Yes. I guess that may be one reason why they—" She bumped into the staircase railing and emitted a startled gasp.

"You seem a little jumpy," Hylan observed, still moving forward.

"No. No. I, um—" Nikki scrambled around the railing and then proceeded to back her way up the stairs. "I'm just a little nervous here."

"I don't blame you," Hylan said, sounding almost sympathetic to her plight.

"Y-you don't?"

"No." He followed her up the staircase. "I've never been arrested before."

"Arrested?"

"Well, don't quote me on this, but masquerading as my wife has a strong whiff of criminality about it. Let's see, you've been living in my house for what?"

"Um, about eighteen months."

Incredulous, Hylan blinked at her. "You've been telling people that we've been married for a year and half?"

Nikki tried to work the quick calculations in her head, but it was hard to concentrate with Hylan glaring at her. "Something close to that."

"And they believed you?"

"Well, you are a busy man and I sort of really wanted

to get away from our jet-setting lifestyle to write a new play. Of course you didn't want me to come here all by myself, but I persuaded you that this was something that I really wanted to do. You know to stop and really just concentrate on the play that's going to launch me onto Broadway."

Hylan froze at the center of the staircase and just stared her.

Nikki continued. "But then I got here and I was hit with a major case of writer's block. Which was true, you know," she added for good measure. "Of course, you call every evening, wondering when I'm coming back stateside. This past winter, you even threatened to divorce me. But after I nearly had an emotional breakdown, you relented and said that I could take all the time I wanted to complete my play." Then she perked up. "Which is almost done, by the way."

Silence.

Nikki crouched back as she struggled to read him again.

Finally Hylan said, "There is something *seriously* wrong with you."

Nikki's heart dropped into the pit of her stomach. "Why?"

"Why?" he thundered. "You've been fabricating a marriage for eighteen months to a man you have never met! Does that sound sane to you? I have family here for Pete's sake."

"Oh, I know. I *adore* your Aunt Addie. She's really been a doll to me since I've been here. You know she says that she hasn't seen you since you were a child. You really should take the time to visit your family more often. Not just, you know—" she shrugged "—bring different girlfriends here to make out on the beach."

Silence.

Nikki coughed and cleared her throat. "Just a suggestion."

"Lady. I don't know who you are and I don't care to know. But I do want you to pack your things and get out of my house. Now!"

Nikki jumped at his sudden roar, and then in the next second jumped again when a thunderclap seemed to shake the house at its very foundation.

Hylan closed his eyes and cursed under his breath. "All right. Make it first thing in the morning."

Nikki sputtered to say something, but the huge lump that had just lodged in the center of her throat prevented any response.

Hylan turned around, grabbed his bags from the foyer and then marched back up the stairs. As he maneuvered past Nikki, who was still standing silently in the center of the staircase, he issued one final warning. "Believe me, if you're still here when I wake up in the morning, I *will* call the police."

Chapter 6

The moment the sky's thick, gray clouds swallowed the evening sun, Saint Lucia was hammered with high winds and sheets of hard-pounding rain. Storms were not unusual from June to December, but after a couple of hours Hylan wondered if they were in the midst of hurricane weather. Why didn't he check the weather forecast before he left Atlanta?

Briefly, he thought to ask his loony tunes, fake wife what they were in for, but then he would quickly dismiss the notion. Mainly because, to add insult to injury, he was forced to huddle up in one of the guestrooms so she could pack up her stuff in the master bedroom.

His room.

In fact, every time his thoughts turned toward the unhinged beauty, he experienced an unsettling tic in his right eye. What kind of woman just moves into a stranger's house and pretends that she's married to him? *A crazy one,* he thought, answering his own question. Hell, maybe he should lock his door and sleep with some kind of weapon under his pillow. Knowing psycho, she could creep into his room, kill him and then pretend to be a widow.

Hylan laughed and then caught himself. What the hell? Was insanity contagious? Seeing how his luck was running lately, it probably was.

Still, the look on her face when their eyes met this afternoon kept eliciting a chuckle or two as he lay across his bed. The kicker was her total commitment to her performance. The way she ran down those stairs and threw her arms around his neck as if she was truly welcoming her husband back home indicated that she had definitely improved on her acting skills since the last time he'd seen her.

And that kiss.

Whew! Hylan shook his head as a sudden heat wave blazed up his neck. He never kept a running tab or anything, but he'd kissed his share of women, and he could honestly say that Ms. Few-Beers-Shy-of-a-Six-Pack was a damn good kisser—and was it just his imagination or did she really taste like…raspberry Bubble Yum?

Who cares what she tasted like? She's crazy.

Funny thing was the more he said it, the more he didn't quite believe it. Well, not completely. There was something else that was going on. He saw it in her eyes when she was rambling on about their near divorce.

Wait a minute. He sat up in bed. Eighteen months ago? Wasn't that about the same time he'd seen her in that play? He tried to do the calculations in head, but was unsure exactly when he'd seen the play. He remembered he'd been seeing Shonda at the time because she was the only one dragging him to theaters that far off Broadway.

"Strange," he mumbled under a sudden clap of thunder. Hylan sat fixed on the side of the bed mulling over this strange twist of fate—or growing list of coincidences. He hadn't decided which one it was just yet. Maybe he was a little harsh on her. He could have sat her down and let her tell him her story from the beginning. Come tomorrow he was going to have one hell of a job, trying to clear up this whole mess.

He tried to picture Rafiq and Mahina's reactions when he told them the news that Nikki was nothing more than an impostor and she had snowed them completely. Truthfully, he couldn't imagine Mahina taking the news all that well. She boasted every chance she could that she was an excellent judge of character and it was clear that she loved Nikki to death.

Now why is that my problem? I'm not the one who lied.

But he was the one kicking her out.

Hylan's head jerked toward his closed door and while the thunder rolled outside, he sat there. Thinking…

In the master bedroom, Nikki had collapsed in a heap in her beloved walk-in closet, sobbing her eyes out. It didn't matter how many times she told herself that she should consider herself lucky that she wasn't sitting in jail right now or that Hylan…or rather Mr. Dawson… had every right to kick her out of this beautiful house— even in the middle of this storm, if he chose to, she still couldn't help but feel wronged somehow. Really. Would it have hurt him to hear her out—to let her explain what happened?

Nikki shoved a pair of her favorite flats against the wall and continued to sulk. What was she going to do now? Where was she going to go—back home?

The very idea caused her eyes to damn near roll to the back of her head. She could just hear her father now. *"When are you going to grow up? When are you going to stop this whole writing nonsense?"*

Another river of tears flowed down her face. This time she didn't bother to try to wipe them away. Maybe it was time for her to give up the ghost—stop chasing rainbows and join the real world. It took some work but she finally managed to pull herself off the floor. Instead of pulling her clothes off each hanger, she simply opened her arms wide and grabbed as much as she could in one fell swoop and then carried them back into the adjoining bedroom. There she proceeded to just dump all of her stuff in an open suitcase in the middle of the huge platform bed. Once she did that the tears came again.

C'mon, girl. Get it together.

The problem with Nikki crying so much meant that hiccups were never too far behind. Was it weird? Yes. But what could she do about it? She hiccupped when she cried. None of it changed the fact that come morning, she would be homeless. Hell, she didn't even have enough to afford a ticket home…and she was *not* calling her parents.

You could call Barbara.

Yeah! She could call her little sister to come to her rescue. *Yippee, yippee, joy, joy.*

In between sniffling and hiccupping, Nikki's gaze veered over to the glowing screen of her laptop on her desk. Well, technically it was Mr. Dawson's desk. She walked toward it as her bottom lip grew heavier. She was so close. About fifteen more pages and she would finally be able to type the words *the end*. In the bigger scheme of things, she guessed that it really didn't matter. It wasn't like there was some big-time producer, salivating for her next script or a swell of fans camped out in long lines at the box office anxiously anticipating opening night.

So what was the big deal?

She wiped her eyes, sniffed and hiccupped. The simple truth was that now was as good a time as any to stop running from reality.

Boom!

Crash!

Nikki screamed at the cannon-like thunder clap, but the crash was definitely a window or something in the house breaking. Without hesitation, she pivoted toward the bedroom door and raced out into the hallway. Then two things happened at once—the lights went out and she smacked into something solid at full speed.

Another scream ripped from her throat. In the next second her ass hit the floor—hard.

"Ouch!"

"I can't tell which is making a louder racket—you or the storm."

Nikki stiffened. Was he mocking her? "What was that noise?" she asked, climbing up from the floor. Not until she was back on her feet and Hylan's hand brushed against her right breast, did she know that he had been trying to offer her his hand in the darkness. The contact was brief, but it was long enough to send a white-hot jolt through her body.

"Oh, excuse me," he said, jerking his hand back.

"It's okay," she whispered, dropping her head and wondering about the lingering tingle from his brief touch.

Bang! Bang!

Nikki jumped again, but she didn't dare scream. The last thing she wanted him to think was that she was some kind of damsel in distress. She was, but she didn't want *him* to know it.

"What the hell is that?" he asked, agitated.

"It's gotta be one of the windows downstairs," she answered, taking off for the stairs. Despite it being pitch black, Nikki navigated her way through the hallway and down the stairs easily. Having been in charge of the renovations, she knew exactly where everything was.

Hylan was a different story.

Nikki was halfway down the staircase when there was a different kind of bang behind her. It was followed by a grunt, a groan and then another bang.

"Goddamn it," he hissed. "Who in the hell put this damn desk right here!"

"Are you all right?" she shouted back at him.

Hylan muttered a few more curses and then it sounded as if he was…hopping.

"Be careful. The staircase brass ball is—"

Thump!

"Aaagh!" Hylan stumbled down the staircase like an avalanche.

Nikki tried to get out of the way, but it was too late. Hylan clipped her at the knees and she landed in his lap, riding him the rest of the way down—screaming all the way. Seconds later, which felt like hours, the bumpy ride came to an abrupt halt, but it took a while for Nikki to realize it. Her life was still flashing before her eyes.

Feeling his nerves being severed, Hylan smacked a hand across her opened mouth. "Damn, girl. You have a set of pipes on you."

She shut up and then wondered what the hell was piercing her so hard in the ass. Then it hit her. "Oh."

"I'm going to remove my hand. Do you promise not to scream my damn ear off?"

Nikki nodded. The moment his hand fell away, she popped out of his lap like a Pop Tart in a toaster. Now she was tingling in a couple of places.

Bang! Bang!

"The window," she whispered and started to take off again.

"Oh, you're just going to leave a brother all busted up on the floor. It's like that?"

"Sorry." Embarrassed, Nikki blindly reached out her hands until she found him struggling to get up. She pulled and tugged, and didn't really believe that she was all that much help in getting him to his feet. "Are you all right?"

Hylan hissed. "Yeah. I think I just aggravated an old basketball injury." When he was finally back on his feet, he said, "After you."

To save time, Nikki grabbed his hand. That same electricity hit her again and she wondered if the man was a walking, talking power grid. "Let's go." She led him by the hand, successfully maneuvering him around plants and furniture with ease. The broken window was in the entertainment room. A tree branch had shattered the glass and one lone shutter kept banging back and forth in the wind.

"I'll go get the nails, drill gun and flashlight," Nikki said. "You stay right here. I'll be right back."

Before Hylan could respond, she was off. A few minutes later, she was back with the tools and more. Feeling the need to prove that he did at least know a little sumthin' sumthin' about maintenance and repair—after all, he was a civil engineer—Hylan grabbed the nails and drill and instructed Nikki where to point the flashlight. It wasn't exactly easy work with all the wind and rain, and by the time he'd removed the fallen tree branch and boarded up the window, he was drenched from head to toe.

"There. That ought to hold it," he panted.

"What's that?" Nikki asked, focusing the light on his left hand. "You're bleeding."

Hylan blinked at the long gash in the palm of his hand. He hadn't even felt it when he'd cut himself.

Nikki clasped his wrist and ignored the bizarre jolt of electricity to lean in for a closer look. "It doesn't look too deep." She shook her head. "Let me fix you up."

Hylan hesitated when she pulled his arm.

She chuckled. "C'mon. I might be a little crazy, but I promise, I'm harmless."

He smiled and allowed her to drag him along, but given how his heart was hammering inside his chest, he wasn't buying that harmless crap one bit.

Chapter 7

Nicole Jamison was crazy—but she was sort of that cute kind of crazy, Hylan decided. For the past twenty minutes, they sat in the center of the living room floor, completely surrounded by an army of candles. After watching her carefully and patiently tend to his cut with a first aid kit he didn't know he owned, he started to feel a little guilty about the way he'd treated her earlier. Not to mention, she had the softest pair of hands he'd ever felt. And what was that delightful scent clinging to her skin?

"There," she said, smiling at her handiwork. "That ought to hold you until you can see Dr. Walcott."

"Is he still practicing?"

"Yep. Cataracts, glaucoma and senility be damned."

Hylan chuckled as he squinted down at his bandaged hand. "Nice work," he said, impressed.

"You say that now, but wait until the lights come back on."

They laughed, their tone blending harmoniously until both remembered that they weren't supposed to like one another. Immediately, their gazes dropped and then shifted around the room.

"Well," Nikki said. "I guess I better get this stuff cleaned up." She grabbed the used cotton balls and unused bandages and started shoving them into a plastic bag.

"Here. Let me help you," Hylan offered.

"No. That's not necessary," Nikki said, rushing to move things out of his way.

"C'mon. I insist."

"It's all right. I got it." She gathered everything and then jumped to her feet, but before she could run away, Hylan caught hold of her dress hem.

"Whoa. Whoa. Slow down," he ordered.

Nikki froze and then slowly allowed her gaze to find him with the aid of the flickering candlelight. *Damn. He's handsome*. His dark mocha skin was now radiant with a luminous golden glow and his eyes exuded warmth that was both thrilling and inviting. This was the face of the ladies' man that she'd heard endless stories about—not the fire-breathing dragon that had ordered her out of the house by morning.

"Sit down," he said, smiling.

She hesitated. True it was a simple request, but suddenly she didn't know whether she could handle a man like Hylan. He had the look of someone who was used to getting what he wanted in life—and right now, he looked as though he wanted her.

The thought was so ludicrous that Nikki laughed aloud at herself.

Hylan frowned and pulled back.

Great. Now he thinks you're crazy again. Nikki bit the bullet and sat back down. Now a strange awkwardness had settled its way into the room and the two strangers were left to listen to the howling wind and relentless rain. It would have helped if Nikki knew how to act around men of Hylan's ilk—or men in general. Another curse in Nikki's life was her uncanny ability to drive men away. *In droves.*

It wasn't her looks. She'd had her fair share of admirers over the years. It was more like…her mouth. Any time she was around a guy she liked, she had two modes: shy—which usually meant that her tongue was so twisted up that she couldn't get the right words to flow—or Chatty Cathy—which meant she couldn't shut up even if someone held a gun to her head and threatened to blow her away. Either way, both responses had the same results—men treated her like she'd just landed from outer space. With all that going on, it was amazing that she'd ever been kissed, much less gotten laid—which, after sex, was when she really got chatting.

Why not, since sex usually lasted all of two minutes.

"Look," Hylan started. "About this afternoon—"

"No. No. You don't have to explain," she said.

"It's just that—"

"You weren't expecting to find someone living in your house," she finished for him.

"Well, I certainly wasn't expecting to find a *wife*."

"Yeah, I guess that was probably a bit of a shock," she acknowledged.

"It's not that I don't think you...you know—wouldn't make a nice wife for someone," he added hesitantly.

"Just not for you," she said, attempting to help.

"Well, I don't really know you," he said, softening his reply with a lighthearted laugh.

"Good point," she added, chuckling and waving a finger at herself.

For a moment, it seemed as if they were on a good roll and breaking the ice, but there was really nowhere to go with this particular line of discussion—not without carelessly tossing the words *crazy, insane, psychotic* or *mentally unbalanced* around. So after another few minutes of listening to the storm, Nikki chose the only other avenue that was left.

"I'm sorry," she said. Unfortunately, it was so low that Hylan didn't quite catch it.

"What?" he asked leaning closer.

Nikki forced her gaze to meet his again. "I owe you a huge apology," she said a little louder. "And I'm really thankful that you didn't drop a dime on me when Momma Mahina and Rafiq were here." Tears stung her eyes before flooding her vision. "That would've been humiliating." She sniffled and wiped a knuckle across the bottom of her lashes.

Hylan sat quietly, watching her.

"I really didn't mean to cause any harm, it's just that…" She glanced away.

Without thinking, Hylan reached over and brushed the thick curtain of black hair from her shoulder. What he uncovered was a beautiful long neck that he was willing to bet everything in his bank account was as sweet as anything Godiva put in a box. "It's just what?"

"I needed to get away," Nikki confessed.

Concerned, Hylan frowned. "Are you in some kind of trouble?"

She shook her head. "I wasn't in any physical danger. I-I guess I was at crossroad in my life and…like my father always says, I chose to run away from it."

"But…why me? Why here?" he asked, his hand still stroking her hair. Even through the candlelight he was able to see her embarrassment in her coloring.

"A, um, former girlfriend of yours had mentioned this place one night at a club. Hell, I don't think I even caught her name," she recalled. "Anyway, I was depressed. I had just become the laughingstock of Broadway—well, not quite Broadway—off Broadway."

You might want to add a few more offs to that, Hylan thought.

"Anyway, I was having a hard time facing the end of…a dream." Her tears came roaring back. "You see, I spent my whole life chasing this ridiculous pot of gold at the end of a rainbow and I just couldn't believe that after pouring everything I had and everything my parents had into this production that it opened and closed practically at the same time. It wasn't supposed to happen like that. It…it wasn't fair."

Hylan's heart lurched. He could see that she was struggling to summon a modicum of dignity, but having been there on her opening night, he knew just how humiliated she'd been. "Nothing in life is fair," he said, gently.

His clichéd response was met with an instant eye roll. "Said the man who has *everything*." She swept her hand around of the room. "Look at this place. It's an island paradise that sits empty for years at a time. You have a business that's booming even in the middle of a recession and—"

"You've been keeping tabs on me?" he asked.

Another wave of color washed over Nikki's face. "Well, people are always asking about…"

"Your husband?"

Instead of answering, she pressed her lips together and nodded sheepishly.

Hylan stopped stroking her hair and inched away again. "I still don't get it."

"It's simple, really. I needed a place to go and I heard that you rarely came here. I figured I'd come, clear my mind, figure out some sort of plan and get out of here before you showed up."

"But you've been here for a year and a half," he said, shaking his head. "Isn't your family looking for you?"

"No. They know where I am. They can't wait to meet you, by the way."

Hylan's frown deepened as he waved a finger at her. "See. When you say stuff like that it scares me."

"Well, I didn't want them to worry and since I had already told people here that I was married, I figured that it would be easier to just keep track of one lie than a whole slew—but it didn't quite work out that way, either." She huffed, exasperated. "Once I got here, it turned out the house wasn't exactly as empty as your ex-girlfriend led me to believe."

"Mahina," he said.

Nikki laughed at a sudden memory. "Swear to God I think we both damn near had a heart attack when she walked in on me in your shower that first morning. There I was thinking that I had died and gone to heaven in that huge marbled and glass shower and when I stepped out in my birthday suit, she was right there ready to knock me into the middle of next week with a cast-iron skillet."

Hylan barely heard anything after the image of her standing naked in his shower popped into his head. "So, um, what did you do?" He coughed, but couldn't clear the sudden thickness clogging his throat or erase the picture of soap bubbles running down her curves.

"Well, I had to think fast. That's for sure. She really looked like she knew how to use that skillet," Nikki said. "She was yelling at me in English, French, Spanish and a few more languages I'm still not sure of, but the gist of it was that I needed to tell her who the hell I was before she called the cops."

"So you told her you were my wife," Hylan said, finally seeing the big picture.

"Well, at first I was trying to say that I had permission to be here."

Hylan cocked his head.

"But it was clear that she wasn't buying that story so I…um, guess I just said the first thing that popped into my head," she said, shrugging her shoulders. "I know it was wrong. Maybe I just got scared for a moment," she reasoned. "But the next thing I knew she was sweeping me up into her arms and swinging me around the room. You had her convinced that you'd never get married."

And she was right, he thought, but refrained from saying it aloud.

"Anyway, she was whooping and hollering so loud that her sisters and your Aunt Addie came running into the room."

Hylan frowned.

"They were all here to cook for a church fundraiser," she supplied. "Next thing I know I was being passed around from one woman to another each of them coming dangerously close to breaking me in half."

"Were you still naked?"

Nikki blinked at the strange question. "Uh, no. I managed to grab a towel when the herd of women came running into the bathroom."

Hylan shook the image of Nikki naked out of his head and tried to concentrate on the point at hand. "Okay. You were caught flat-footed breaking into my house so you lied."

She looked insulted. "I was caught taking a shower and I avoided going to jail," she amended. "Really, I don't see what the big deal is. It's not like I snuck in here to rob you blind or anything. There was no harm done."

"Except you were living here rent- and utility-free. And no doubt you've been using the house expense accounts for food, clothes and whatever else you needed to maintain your new identity," he tacked on. "Some would say—me in particular—*that* was a form of stealing."

Nikki jerked away from him. "Wait a minute. I didn't just lounge around here like the Queen of Sheba, you know. I worked very hard on this property. I scrubbed and cleaned and helped Momma Mahina with most of her duties. When that hurricane blew through here last fall, I took charge of renovating the place—and some would say—*me in particular*—that I did a damn good job, too."

Seeing that she was dead serious, Hylan stared incredulously at her.

"And stop looking at me like that," she snapped, feeling her nerves fray. "I'm not crazy. I did what I did out of desperation, but it's not like I killed someone— and it's not like you didn't benefit from it."

"Is that right?"

"Hell, yeah that's right. Before I married you, people around here had a very low opinion of you, you know. You're related to maybe half the people in the quarter and yet you never come to visit—and when you do, it's to parade your latest, empty-headed but always half-naked girlfriend on the beach. You don't call, you don't write, but when you do show up it's to parade around like some proud peacock. News flash—your money doesn't impress anybody around here."

Now Hylan was insulted. "What? I'm supposed to be ashamed of my accomplishments?"

"No, but you could give back the very thing they gave you during those summer months when you were growing up."

"And what was that?"

"Love," she said simply.

Hylan's heart kicked at the mention of the word. He liked the way it sounded coming from her lips. "You know a lot about that, do you?"

"What, love?" she asked.

He smiled.

"Maybe," she said, shrinking back.

"Aw." Hylan nodded and folded his arms. "Real easy to lecture me, isn't it, *Mrs. Dawson?* What's your relationship with your family like?"

Nikki started to scramble back to her feet, but Hylan quickly wrapped an arm around her shoulder and restrained her. "Where are you going, sweetheart? I thought we were trying to get to know each other. After all, it seems that you know an awful lot about me."

"Well…just what people here have told me. The rest I sort of just made up."

"Made up, eh?" Hylan couldn't believe he was starting to find this whole thing amusing. "Like what?"

She started squirming. "Just…how we met and how you proposed to me."

"Oh, this ought to be good," he said, turning and

giving her his complete, undivided attention. "Exactly how *did* we meet?"

Nikki squirmed a bit. "Well, you, um…came to one of my plays."

Hylan's brows spiked in surprise. "Did I now?"

She nodded. "And you loved it, by the way."

"Of course I did."

"One of the best plays you'd seen in a long time, you said." Her eyes rolled upward as if she was imagining the whole scenario. "I thanked you and told you how much I really appreciated your coming to see it. But even as we shook hands there was an instant spark between us. Everyone saw it—including your date that evening."

"Ah. So you stole me from another woman?"

She shrugged. "Well, she was sort of on the bimbo-ish side."

"So my usual fare?"

Nikki nodded. "She just kept standing there, twirling her hair, popping her gum and asking me how come there weren't any poles on the stage."

Hylan laughed so hard his head nearly rocked off his shoulders.

"Anyway, for the next two weeks during the play's run you were right there in the front row, laughing at every joke and leading the crowd in a standing ovation."

"That's the kind of guy I am."

"You were so sweet," she gushed. "After every performance you'd come backstage with a dozen roses, congratulating me on another great performance. And each night you would ask me out, but I would always turn you down."

"Why?"

"I had a boyfriend," she said.

"First time I've heard of a boyfriend," he said, disappointed. "Who is this guy?"

"Oh, I just made him up," she said with a casual wave.

"Figures..."

"What? It was perfectly reasonable for me to play hard to get."

"Why? If you like someone, you should go out with them. Why play games?" He ground his teeth together. "Women!"

"Oh, right! Like men don't play games. In fact that's all you ever do—*especially* you."

"Oh, are we back to what people *told* you about me or are we dealing with facts yet?"

"Okay, then. You tell me why you haven't settled down—or why you're attracted to women who are allergic to clothes."

"So because I don't want to get married that makes me a bad guy?"

"What's wrong with getting married? To have and to hold someone until death do you part?"

"Why should I limit my options?"

"You mean you can't keep your dick in your pants, don't you?" she sassed back, smugly.

"My dick is not the issue." Hylan couldn't believe that he was having this discussion.

"When it comes to men, their dicks are *always* the issue."

"I resent that."

"But you don't deny it?"

Hylan was boxed in. He had the feeling that if he gave her an answer, any answer, that she'd flip it and make him sound like some serial womanizer—who needed to be put down in order to save mankind—or womankind. "You know what? I'm not going to answer that."

"Smart man."

"Wait. How come *you're* not married? Oh, wait. I forgot. You're too busy pretending to be married to men you've never met before."

Nikki gasped.

He actually felt guilty for striking the low blow.

"I could get married if I wanted to," she said.

"Yeah. Okay." Hylan decided that it was best to let that one go.

"What? Are you suggesting that a man wouldn't want to marry me?"

"No. I'm not saying that at all." He tried to backpedal his way out of the conversation.

"Because I could, you know." Her confident statement was undermined by her lowered chin and slumping shoulders. "It's just that…well, you know the life of a writer is very solitary…and I was really focused on my career."

"The one that blew up in your face?"

She gasped again, this time tears glistened in her eyes.

"I'm sorry," he said, reaching over and taking her hand. "That was uncalled for," he said.

Their eyes locked. Something, neither knew what it was, started flowing between them—electricity, a moment, a feeling.

Suddenly, Hylan became fascinated with her mouth. It was full, shapely and held the promise of softness and sweetness that was tempting Hylan to do the unthinkable.

"Look, Mr. Dawson—"

"Hylan," he corrected. At her surprised look, he added, "I think it's customary for a wife to call her husband by his first name."

Nikki laughed.

Hylan even liked the way she did that. This whole incident was a shame because under different circumstances, he would probably try to holler at her. "Look. Your relationship with your family is none of my business," he acquiesced. "And maybe there was really no real harm done here. *But* you have to admit this whole thing is a little bizarre."

She nibbled on her bottom lip before finally shrugging and conceding the point.

"And tomorrow when I have to tell—"

"Do you have to?" she asked as if suddenly realizing that the people she'd come to love over the past year were going to find out the truth about her.

"Of course I have to tell them," he said.

"Why? Can't you just tell them that we're, I don't know, um, separating or getting a divorce?"

"What? So they can go back to thinking that *I'm* the bad guy? No thank you."

"So you rather they start hating me?"

"Are you even listening to yourself?" Hylan shook his head.

"Yes. But, it's just that I really adore Momma Mahina and I know that she's not going to take my...my..."

"Deception?"

"Fine." She rolled her eyes. "She's not going to like the fact that I deceived her all this time. You might not know this, but she's a very prideful woman."

"I do know that and you should have thought about it a long time ago." His reprimand caused her bottom lip to start quivering. He relented and gave her shoulder another squeeze. "And don't worry. Mahina never stays mad for long. She'll forgive you...in time."

Nikki dropped her chin and smacked her hand against her forehead. "What was I thinking?"

"No clue."

"Why didn't I leave sooner?"

"You got me."

"Why did *you* come back?"

"I have no—what?" His arm fell away from her shoulders.

"Well our marriage was going great before you showed up."

"Unbelievable." Hylan rolled his eyes and shook his head. "I give up."

Nikki laughed. Even when he glanced at her, she couldn't stop laughing.

Figuring that her last comment was meant as a joke, he joined in, completely loving the way her laughter sounded like music. Before he knew it, he was staring at her mouth again and fighting that animal desire to kiss her. A few seconds later, he could tell that she was fending off the same impulse because her dark gaze had locked onto his own lips.

Then it was just the sound of the rain against the roof and windows that set the mood. When that wasn't enough, gravity wielded its power and the two slowly started leaning toward each other.

Hylan just wanted a taste to satisfy his curiosity. *One kiss, that's all.*

Nikki's brain was screaming for her to snap out of whatever trance this notorious playboy had cast over her, but she couldn't seem to do it. She just wanted one taste to satisfy her own curiosity. *One kiss, that's all.*

But the moment their lips melded together, they were both lost—swept into a different kind of storm that was brewing inside of them. For Hylan, Nikki's lips delivered on their promise. They were softer than anything he'd ever known and just sweet enough to give him a sugar high. For Nikki, she finally understood why women fell for this handsome man. It wasn't the money or power he possessed, but the magic and tenderness of his touch.

There was a loud shriek from the house alarm system and the entire house was flooded with light as the electricity came back on. Even still, Hylan and Nikki were reluctant to break their kiss. It was as if they'd been starving for each other their whole lives.

When it finally dawned on Hylan exactly what he was doing, he pulled back and blinked at the woman in front of him in surprise.

The long stare made Nikki self-conscious and made

her fully realize what she'd just done: made a fool of herself again. She quickly jumped to her feet, and this time he didn't stop her. "I—I guess I better get back upstairs and finish packing."

Hylan opened his mouth, but at the last minute decided that it was best to let her go.

"Right," she said and then raced out of the room in embarrassment.

Chapter 8

Trees down. Roads closed. Nobody was getting off the island.

Nikki had the sneaking suspicion that Hylan wasn't going to like hearing that when he woke up that morning. As for herself, she was a bit relieved seeing as how she didn't have anywhere to go and she hadn't quite mustered up the courage to call her family for a plane ticket home. The only thing left to do now was to make sure to stay out of Hylan's way until she could leave.

Not only that, she sort of hoped that he wouldn't mind keeping their whole not being married thing between them until after she left. Fat chance of that happening. After last night, she wasn't sure whether she'd been successful in trying to explain why she did what she did and how it all just sort of snowballed—but at least he wasn't yelling at her anymore.

"Good morning."

Nikki's head jerked up from the picnic basket she was cramming with food. Her train of the thought was completely derailed at the sight of Hylan's six-foot-three chocolate, hard body standing in the kitchen doorway dressed in only a pair of black, silk boxers. Damn. The man must live in the gym. His shoulders alone were the size of mountains and his pecs, good Lord, they looked like fine works of art that she would love nothing more than to run her fingers all over. Staring, she could feel her eyes bulge and her mouth sag open.

"Are you robbing the cupboards now?" he asked, smiling.

Nikki snapped her mouth shut. *He sure does know how to ruin a good fantasy.* "I'm not stealing…I'm borrowing," she corrected, stiffening her jaw. "Trees are down, blocking the roads so I figured that I'd walk this basket over to Momma Mahina just in case she needs anything."

Hylan strolled over to the kitchen counter, stopped next to her and took a peek inside the basket. "Homemade biscuits, sausage links, bacon, eggs and what's this?" He peeled back the foil on a plate. "Pancakes?" His gaze shifted to hers. "When I smelled all that cooking you were doing, I thought it was for me."

"You? Why would I be cooking for you?"

He chuckled. "I don't know. Maybe to try and butter me up to let you stay here since the roads are down."

Hell. I hadn't thought about that.

"Maybe you just didn't think about it," he said, as if he'd heard her private thoughts.

She shrugged and shifted away from him, mainly because his aftershave was doing a number on her endorphins. "I didn't know what kind of food you liked."

"I'm a man. I'll eat pretty much anything you put in front of me." He reached into the basket and pinched off a piece of bacon.

"I'll keep that in mind," Nikki said, struggling to keep her eyes averted from his chest. Instead she kept catching glimpses of his incredible six-pack abs that looked hard enough to grate cheese on.

"You know, in all the years that I've known Mahina, I've never known her *not* to have food in her house." He reached inside the basket again, but was surprised when she popped him on the hand for his efforts. "Hey!"

"She does have food, that's not the point," she said, closing the basket.

"Taking food to someone that has food sounds a bit—"

"Don't say it," she warned, waving a finger. "I'm *not* crazy."

Hylan tossed his hands up in the air. "I wasn't going to say it."

Her eyes narrowed in a way that called him a liar.

"I was just going to say that it was a bit...*odd*."

Nikki rolled her eyes and snatched the basket away from him. "It's just a gesture to let her know that we were thinking about her—well, at least I was."

"What—are you trying to say that I wasn't concerned?"

"Were you?"

He blinked. "Well, I, um, haven't given it much
thought yet. I mean, I did just wake up."

"Uh-huh." She hooked the basket on her arm and
prepared to walk off.

"Wait. What about me?"

Nikki frowned and jabbed a fist against her hip.
"What about you?"

He stood there blinking. "Well, I'm hungry."

"Then fix yourself something to eat. What do I look
like—your maid?"

Hylan shook his head as he stormed toward the
cupboard. "Jeez. Some wife you are. I don't know why
the hell I married you." When his words processed
through his head, he stopped short and then glanced
over to see Nikki smirking at him. "Great. Now I'm
losing it."

Okay. So the food wasn't *just* an "I was worried about
you" sort of gesture. Hylan was right. Momma Mahina
usually had more food than the local grocery store.
The truth was more like Nikki hoped that making her
friend a home-cooked meal would soften the blow of
her confession. She woke up thinking that if the truth
had to come out, then maybe it would be best if Momma
Mahina heard it from her.

There was no guarantee of that, of course. She had
seen the older woman's temper in the past and there
was a reason why most people prayed to never get on

her bad side. The woman wouldn't hesitate to swing a skillet at anyone—Reverend Oxford learned that the hard way.

"Oh, my goodness," Momma Mahina exclaimed when she looked up from sweeping her front porch. "I don't believe you chile." She set the broom aside and rushed down the stairs. "What are you doing trampling through all this mess?"

"I just came to check and see how you guys weathered the storm last night," Nikki said almost sheepishly. "And I brought you this."

Mahina's look of surprise quickly morphed into confusion. "Oh, honey. You know that thing was nothing but a baby compared to what we usually get this time of year," she laughed, but accepted Nikki's kind gesture with a smile. "Now you get on back and take care of that husband of yours. After so much time apart, I'm amazed that you two even noticed that storm last night."

Nikki flushed as she remembered the intoxicating kiss she and Hylan shared last night. Without realizing it, a soft smile curled her lips and her eyes had a faraway look.

"Ooh. Now that's what I'm talking about." Mahina swung and bumped her hip against Nikki's.

Unfortunately, Nikki wasn't prepared for it and stumbled a full foot away from the woman. "Hey," she chuckled. "Careful where you swing those hips."

Momma Mahina rocked her head back with a hearty laugh as she headed back up the porch stairs. "Whatcha need to do is put a little more meat on those bones," she said. "Men like having something to hold on to, ain't that right, Lathan?" she asked her husband as he stepped out onto the porch.

"Damn right," he agreed though both women knew that he had no clue as to what they were talking about.

Nikki laughed.

Mahina stopped to stare at her husband while he struggled to strap on his tool belt. "And now where do you think you're going?"

"I'm going to fix that roof," he said. "It looks like we have our own waterfall in the center of the living room."

Mahina rolled her eyes. No way was she going to let her seventy-eight-year-old husband climb up on the roof. "Are you crazy? You're going up there so you can break that old, fool neck of yours. I haven't paid the life insurance this month. Wait until Rafiq gets here. He will take care of it."

Lathan looked wounded. "I don't need to wait for that knuckleheaded boy. I know how to fix my own roof."

"No, Lathan. Now come on in here and fix yourself a plate of this good food Nikki brought over." She waltzed on into the house.

Lathan rolled his eyes.

"I saw that!" Mahina shouted as if she had eyes in the back of her head.

Lathan looked at Nikki, but all she could do was shrug her shoulders and mouth the words, *I'm sorry.*

His eyes sparkled as if he finally realized who she was and then he shuffled down the stairs. "Ah, darlin' Nikki. What chu doin' here?" He looked around. "Now,

I know Hylan wasn't crazy enough to let you out of his sight so soon." He took her into his thin arms and embraced her.

Nikki adored Lathan, but she could swear that the man was nothing but skin and bones.

"Nikki. Lathan. Get on in here while I heat this food up."

"Coming," they shouted unison. They looked at each other and smiled.

"We better go on in there before she gets that skillet after us," Lathan said, leading Nikki into the house.

The moment she entered the house, Nikki saw that they had, in fact, suffered damages in last night's storm. It was just like Mahina to cover up and pretend that she didn't need help. And just like countless times before, Nikki wasted no time getting right to work.

However, Lathan dove right into the basket Nikki brought over. "I know I smell pancakes and biscuits in here."

Momma Mahina just shook her head. "Now, he knows he ate just an hour ago."

"Shoot," Lathan said, shoving a strip of bacon into his mouth. "I can always eat. I got plenty of room."

Momma Mahina rolled her eyes and went back to cleaning up the small house.

For a few minutes they worked harmoniously side but side, but Nikki soon felt the weight of Momma Mahina's gaze on her. The question was in the room without anyone voicing it. Nikki tried to keep her gaze averted, but Mahina's eyes were like magnets. When their eyes finally locked, there was so much love and concern in Mahina's face that tears leapt into Nikki's eyes.

"What's the matter, chile?"

I can't do this, she realized. How could she possibly tell this woman that she's been lying to her for the past year and a half?

"You'll never guess who I found wondering around outside," Rafiq's boisterous voice boomed.

That magnetic connection dissolved and both women's eyes swung toward the front door where both Rafiq and Hylan stood smiling at everyone.

"I figured I'd come over and see if you guys needed any more help. Plus, I heard you guys had breakfast."

"Hylan!" Mahina dropped her broom and clasped her hands together. "You came." She rushed over and wrapped her arms around him.

Rafiq frowned. "What about me? I'm the one that found him."

Momma Mahina just rewarded her nephew's pouting with a quick smack on his arm.

"Ow!" Rafiq said in an overly dramatic tone, acting like he'd just been shot by an AK-47.

"Nikki had me scared there for a minute."

"Oh?" His gaze swept over to Nikki.

She looked away.

Rafiq started sniffing the air. "Is that pancakes I smell?"

"Uh-huh," Lathan mumbled around his stuffed mouth. "Nikki brought it."

Rafiq clapped his hands. "Lord knows I love a woman

who knows their way around the kitchen." He elbowed Hylan. "You're a lucky man."

"That's what you keep telling me." Hylan waited to see if Nikki's gaze would float back to him so he could read exactly how he should play this situation. This whole thing was crazy, but the truth of the matter was that he did sort of feel sorry for her. She was having a serious streak of bad luck. She had been carrying on this charade for a year and a half—what was a couple more days until she left the island?

"You said you didn't have breakfast yet?" Mahina asked, pulling him toward the kitchen.

"Can't say that I have."

"Nikki, chile. Get in that kitchen and fix your man a plate," she ordered. Her tone made it clear that she didn't want to hear any argument.

"Yes, ma'am."

Mahina tsked and shook her head. "I swear I don't know where that girl's head is at."

"Now that Rafiq *and* Hylan are here, they can help me get that roof fixed," Lathan said in between smacking his lips.

"They go on the roof and you stay on the ground," Mahina said, walking to the refrigerator and pulling out a pitcher of juice.

Lathan rolled his eyes.

"I saw that!" Mahina snapped, even though her back was turned away from Lathan.

Nikki slapped a couple of pancakes and biscuits onto a plate and then plopped it down in front of Hylan. "Here."

The kitchen fell silent.

Hylan looked up, amused by her insolent behavior. "Mind if I get some syrup with this?"

Nikki's jaw twitched. She reached across the table, grabbed the bottle of syrup and smacked it next to his plate. "There."

Hylan's smile slid wider. "Butter?"

Nikki rolled her eyes and stomped over to the refrigerator. A frowning Mahina handed her a stick of butter; Nikki accepted it with a smile, but it was quickly erased when she turned back toward the table. "There."

Hylan's eyes started twinkling. "And how about something to eat this wonderful food with, *honey?*"

"Are you for real?" Nikki huffed.

"Chile, what has gotten into you?" Mahina chastised, bringing Hylan a knife and fork. "I've seen farm animals treated better.

Hylan chuckled. "My *wife* is still a little sore at me for me for staying away for so long."

Nikki blinked. She couldn't believe her ears.

"Oh." Mahina relaxed. "Well, I don't blame her for that." She smacked Hylan across the arm.

"Ow. What's with all the hitting?"

"Just be happy it's not my skillet, boy. There's no excuse for such nonsense."

Lathan and Rafiq bobbed their heads as they watched the drama unfolding as if it was the latest summer blockbuster.

"But now that you're home," Mahina continued, "I'm sure that you're going to be able to work everything out because everyone in the quarter knows that this chile loves you."

Hylan's brows jumped at that bit of information. "Is that right?"

"Of course that's right," Mahina carried on. "She has to. The way she would go on and on about you, it couldn't be nothing but love."

Watching the smug and amused look in Hylan's eyes, Nikki wished the floor would just open up and swallow her whole.

"The way you met and the way you proposed," Mahina giggled. "Why I had no idea that you were so romantic. I bet after listening to Nikki's stories all the women in the quarter are in love with you. The single girls and the married ones," she chuckled.

Hylan's ego inflated. "Well, when you have someone as beautiful as my wife, it just comes naturally."

Nikki's neck and face flushed a deep burgundy. It also didn't help that Hylan was looking at her like she was a New York strip steak.

"Uh-huh," Mahina said, catching their open stares. "I think that everything is going to work out *just* fine." She winked at them and returned to her work.

After the men finished their breakfast, Lathan ushered Rafiq and Hylan up on the roof while Mahina and Nikki got busy working in the house and then out in the yard. As usual it was beautiful day—a tad breezy with the promise of rain later that night. For the first few hours, Hylan didn't mind working with his hands, being a civil engineer he knew a little sumthin' about putting things together. However, it seemed like most of the time he was just correcting Rafiq's mistakes, even though Rafiq thought he was doing a bang-up job and couldn't stop crowing about his work.

That afternoon, Momma Mahina ordered everyone off the roof so she and Nikki could serve them some lunch. Of course, she arranged it so that Nikki catered to Hylan.

He couldn't help but be amused and he even got a thrill watching her squirm around him. She looked like a long-tailed cat in a room full of rocking chairs and he was determined to milk the situation for all it was worth. "What's the matter, *sweetie?*" he asked, pulling her down into his lap while she was trying uncap his bottle of Heineken.

"Hey, what are you doing?" she asked, in a whispered panic.

"Hmm? What's the matter?" He nuzzled her neck, loving the scent of mandarin, iris, vanilla and even a hint of sandalwood. "I thought you liked playing make-believe?" His mouth moved over to nibble on her earlobe. "I thought you wanted to convince everyone that we were a happy, loving couple?"

Nikki's eyes dropped low when he found one of her G-spots right behind her ear. "I-It's not that. It's just that…that, oh God." Against the curve of her butt, she could feel the effect she was having on him. To say that she was surprised at just how low he was hanging would have been an understatement.

"Get a room," Rafiq heckled and then barked with laughter.

Jarred back to reality, Nikki sprang up from Hylan's

lap and rushed back into the kitchen. Her face was so red that it looked purple.

Hylan chuckled and continued eating.

"See whatcha done?" Momma Mahina smacked her nephew on the back of the head. "Enough from the peanut gallery."

Lathan shoved another drumstick into his mouth and shook his head. Clearly he knew when to keep his mouth shut.

However, Hylan wasn't through messing around with Nikki. When they all returned to their cleaning up duties, he made sure that at every chance, he would either sneak a kiss, cop a feel or whisper lurid things he wanted to do to her when they returned home. All just so he could watch her squirm like a nervous ninny. Plus, he liked kissing and touching her—which was no surprise. She was a beautiful woman.

A voluptuous woman.

A tempting woman.

And, unfortunately, a crazy woman.

But then again three out of four wasn't too bad.

A few hours later, just when Hylan thought they would be able to call it a day, a Mrs. Lyttle showed up, telling Mahina and Nikki about some damage to her property during the storm, and the next thing Hylan knew they were all headed over to her place.

"Sooo. You finally remembered you had a wife and decided to come back home, did you now?" Mrs. Lyttle asked, her small eyes raking him up and down. "You should be ashamed of leaving a sweet girl like

Nikki here all by herself for so long. I don't care how handsome and rich you are."

Having never met Mrs. Lyttle before, Hylan didn't know how to react to her freely offered opinions.

"Take my word for it, money can't buy you love. And it's clear to everyone with eyes that this woman here loves you."

Hylan pulled Nikki close against his sweat-drenched body. "So everyone keeps telling me. But you don't have to worry, Mrs. Lyttle. A love like ours will triumph over a little thing like distance. I'm hers for as long as she'll have me. Isn't that right, sweetheart?" He pressed a kiss against the top of her forehead.

"Of course, darling." Nikki's heart fluttered. She wished that he would stop grabbing her all willy-nilly. It was playing havoc on her emotions—more so than she would've imagined. But maybe, just maybe, after pretending to be married to the man for so long a small part of her blurred the lines of make-believe. She squirmed out of his arms. "I better go help Momma Mahina," she said and took off.

She heard him chuckling behind her, but she didn't care. She needed to put as much space between them as she possibly could. It was the only way she could think clearly anymore. The fact that she'd brought all of this on herself didn't really help that much. Neither did the fact that he was doing all of this to help her save face. Hell, the whole situation had her confused. She didn't want him to tell anyone the truth, but she couldn't take him pretending to be her loving husband. Nikki had meant it when she said their marriage was better when he wasn't around.

As she helped to lug fallen tree limbs and branches around the property, she continued to try and analyze her screwed-up emotions. How could she not feel the way she was feeling when she'd oohed and aahed over pictures of him as a newborn and from a few years ago with both his cousins and aunts—and even some of the photos he had laying around his vacation home. She knew things about him like that he was a math whiz at age six. His first crush was on Janet Jackson, and his first pet was a turtle named Speedy. Hell, she even knew odd things like he hated peas and spinach, could eat grilled cheese sandwiches until he barfed and hated when people pronounced the "l" in salmon.

It had been easy to make up new stories about their brief courtship and marriage when everyone was so willing to provide such rich background details about the man she claimed to love—or could see herself loving.

Maybe I have lost it.

That was a disturbing thought. Then again, how did people know when they were going crazy? Or maybe the fear of going crazy was enough to drive someone crazy. Too bad there wasn't something like an at-home test kit on the market so she could check these things.

"Did you know that your nose sort of wrinkles up when you're thinking too hard?" Hylan said, appearing out of nowhere as usual.

"What?" She glanced around and saw that everyone was calling it a day.

Hylan jammed his hands into his pants pockets and smiled down at her. "You know you're right. You are a hard worker."

She flashed him a half smile. "Thanks."

"Nah. I mean it. I don't know if you were trying to impress me or you had something to prove to these tree branches."

"I certainly wasn't trying to impress you."

Hylan hiked one brow. "Now why don't I believe that?"

"You really are an egomaniac, aren't you?"

"And you're the prettiest liar I've ever met—but that and a nickel will get us exactly where we are—having this ridiculous conversation."

"Well, please. Don't let me keep you," she tried to storm around him, but his hand whipped out of his pocket and wrapped around her waist so fast that it damn near gave her whiplash.

"Ah, ah, ah. Not so fast, sweetheart," he said, laughing. "There's no way I'm going to let you paint me as the bad guy when we get our divorce."

"Excuse me?" She blinked up at him.

"Well, I've got to tell them something when you leave," he said simply. "Clearly I can't expose you as a liar now that I've been playing along, now can I?"

"I don't believe this," she said shaking her head.

"What? You started this. Are you saying now that you'd rather tell everyone the truth?" Before she could answer, he whipped his head around. "Hey, Mahina! Can you come here for a minute? There's something Nikki would like to tell you."

Nikki panicked and tugged on his arm. "What? Wait! What are you doing?"

"Here I come, baby," Mahina called back.

Hylan frowned. "I thought you wanted to come clean."

"I didn't say that," she hissed. "Never mind, Momma Mahina. Hylan was just playing."

"No I—"

Nikki jumped onto her toes and slapped a hand over Hylan's mouth. "All right. You win. Shut up." She could feel his smile under the palm of her hand.

Hylan pulled her hand down. "Never mind, Mahina!"

Nikki shook her head. "I don't think I like you."

"No? Word around town is that you looove me." He drew her up against his body. "Now you shut up and kiss me."

"What?"

"And make it good. Everyone is watching."

Nikki glanced out of the side of her eyes and saw that they did have a captive audience. Pushing her pride aside, she wrapped her arms around his neck and laid it on him. But she must've forgotten just how intoxicating Hylan's lips were. Within seconds every thought in her head faded away while her body tingled and quivered as if she'd just plugged into an electrical socket.

Their audience broke into spontaneous applause. Rafiq added a few whoops and whistles, but none of that fazed Hylan and Nikki. Their mouths and tongues explored one another with a fever neither had experienced before. When their lips finally pulled apart, they gazed into each other's eyes as if truly seeing each other for the first time. And what they saw scared the hell out of them.

Chapter 9

Later that evening, Nikki and Hylan returned home to a tomb of silence. It was appropriate since the *fake* husband and wife hadn't uttered a word to each other since their very public display of affection. Both knew that they needed to talk about what happened, but right now they needed to get their thoughts together. They retreated to their separate bedrooms and then separate showers.

Standing under a hot stream of water, Hylan tried to remember the last time he'd met someone as complex and fascinating as this woman that was masquerading as his wife. She was surely one of the most beautiful. Today she had worked and toiled with what looked like little to no makeup and she could still easily put models he'd dated or seen on fashion magazine covers to shame.

Maybe it was that quirky personality of hers that made her scared and vulnerable one minute and then strong and sassy the next.

Maybe the woman is just bipolar, he reasoned. *But she sure in the hell can kiss.* That was for damn sure. The first couple of times, he thought it was a fluke. But this last time had him really rethinking a few things. Like, he wouldn't mind getting to know her better. And why not? He was on vacation. He could use some company.

Hylan started warming up to this line of thinking. What would it really hurt if this small corner of the world thought he was married? They had for the past eighteen months anyway. What was a couple of more weeks? He smiled to himself as he started scrubbing his chest.

In the master bathroom, Nikki was thinking the complete opposite. She needed to swallow her pride and call her baby sister to ask for a plane ticket back home. No doubt about it, she had bitten off more than she could chew in dealing with Hylan Dawson. The man had her thinking about things she had never thought about before and feeling things she never felt before—which was *still* crazy, right?

Yet, she was reluctant to leave. She had come to love this house, the friends she had made and even the fantasy she'd created in her mind. She stopped scrubbing her body to think about that.

Unfortunately she stood there thinking too long, because while she had conditioner in her hair and soap lathered on her body, the water went from piping hot

to ice cold in the blink of an eye. "Oh, shit. Shit." She
scrambled, trying to get out of the shower, but not before
a few icicles stabbed her in the back. "Good Lord." She
snatched a towel from the counter and quickly wrapped
it around her shivering body.

When she rushed out of the bathroom, she was
assaulted by a cold blast that raised an entire league
of goose bumps over her body. She knew exactly what
the problem was. The damn pilot light had gone out
on the water heater again. Rafiq had promised her that
he'd fixed it. But, as usual, whatever Rafiq fixed stayed
broken.

Soaking wet, she rushed down two flights of stairs
to reach the basement. At the door, she remembered to
grab a metal pipe she kept against the wall to jimmy the
door. Without it, the door would shut closed and lock
from the outside. That was something else Rafiq was
supposed to fix. The concrete floor was freezing as she
raced toward the water heater and confirmed that the
light was indeed out. "Ah, damn it." She pivoted around
and went over to an old wooden desk across the room
where she knew she kept a box of matches.

"Come on, baby. Light up," she begged as she struck
the match and turned the control knob. Just before she
placed it up to the burner, the basement door burst open
and Hylan stormed into the room. His attire matched
her own—wet skin and a single towel, hugging his hips.
Nikki just barely registered the clang of the metal pipe,
before the door started to swing close. "Catch the door,"
she shouted.

Hylan jerked around and grabbed for the door, but

grasped air instead as the door shut with a loud bang. He tried again and clasped the metal knob where he pulled and tugged. But it was no use. It was locked.

Nikki groaned but then the small flame in her hand burned her fingers and she dropped the match. "Please. Please. Don't say we're locked in here," she begged, jumping to her feet and running over to the door.

Hylan swore under his breath as he turned away, but Nikki kept pulling and tugging in a fit of denial.

"No. No. No. How are we going to get out of here?" she cried.

"Calm down." Hylan exhaled a long breath, but then started to look around. "There's got to be another way out of here."

Nikki finally gave up and collapsed against the door. "There isn't," she groaned. "Believe me. I know."

Hylan turned and looked at her. "You've been trapped down here before?"

Nikki lowered her face into her hands and groaned, "Twice."

There was a long stretch of silence while the severity of their situation settled in. "So...we're trapped in here?"

She nodded.

"Together?" he said for further clarification.

Nikki dropped her hands and glared up at him. "Yes, Einstein. We are trapped down here *together*—until somebody notices we're missing and comes looking for us. Is that clear enough for you or do you need me to draw a picture?"

"All right. No need to get testy," he said, determined

to remain calm. But when he started thinking just how long it could be before anyone thought to come and look for them, his chest tightened with anxiety. "What's the longest you've been down here?"

"Three days," she croaked.

Hylan needed to sit down. With half the island thinking that they needed time to reunite after being separated for so long they could easily be down here a week or two. "This is not happening." He shot back over to the door.

Nikki had just barely scrambled out of the way when he started banging away. "Hey, anybody out there! We're stuck down here!" Bang! Bang! Bang!

"Now who's crazy? Who are you yelling at? There's nobody here in the house but us."

Bang! Bang! Bang!

"Hello!"

"Hell, maybe we both need straightjackets," Nikki concluded, walking back over to the water heater and grabbing the box of matches she'd discarded.

Hylan turned away from the door and eyed her wearily. "What are you doing?"

"Finishing what I came down here to do. It's either that or help you shout at imaginary people."

"You're a regular comedian. Maybe you should give up being a playwright and try out for *Last Comic Standing* or something."

"Ha-ha."

"Oh. I forgot. You get stage fright."

"What?"

Hylan clamped his mouth shut, realizing that he

had said too much. "Nothing. I'm just…frustrated," he admitted before kneeling in front of the door.

"What? You're going to start praying now?"

"Ha-ha. You're on a roll tonight." He ran a finger around the doorknob. "No. I'm trying to check out the screws on this thing. There's gotta be some tools down here, right? We can just take the whole knob off and… voila!"

"Tools are outside in the shed where they always are."

Hylan dropped his head. "After getting trapped down here *twice* you didn't think to keep something down here to make sure that you didn't get stuck again?"

"Yes. That was what the metal pipe was for. You're the one who barged in here and knocked it loose."

"I came to see why the shower turned into Antarctica," he reasoned as he climbed back up onto his feet. "Forgive me since I didn't know that I needed to be watchful of a metal pipe jimmying the door."

"Well now you know." She drew in a deep breath and rolled her eyes. "Look. I don't want to fight. I'm cold. I'm tired. I'm wet."

Hylan snickered.

"Nice." Nikki folded her arms. "Get your head out of the gutter."

He held up his hands. "Sorry."

Nikki lit the pilot light, stood and tightened the towel across her chest before moving back over to the old desk. The basement temperature was a concern. Her hair was already feeling like a curtain of ice.

"Are you okay?" he asked, genuinely concerned.

She nodded as she eased up on the corner of the desk and hugged her arms around her. "I'm just a little cold, that's all."

Hylan glanced around in search of something to keep her warm and then down at his own towel.

"Don't even think about it," she warned.

"I was just trying to be a gentleman."

"Sure you were." Nikki laughed, but in the back of her mind she was beyond curious to see what he had hidden under that towel. With that chest, those abs and powerful legs, she had no reason to doubt that his entire body wasn't a work of art.

"Looks like my mind isn't the only one in the gutter," he said.

She realized that he'd caught her staring and looked away. She tensed when Hylan strolled over and sat on the desk beside her. He smelled wonderful, like sandalwood and musk. Trying to be inconspicuous, Nikki closed her eyes and inhaled softly.

"It's specially made," he said.

Her eyes sprang back open. "What?"

"The soap," he said, smiling. "You were sniffing me, weren't you?"

"Was not," she protested too loudly.

He tossed up his hands and rolled his eyes. "Ookay." Clearly, he didn't believe her.

"You're impossible."

He smirked. "By the way, you smell nice, too."

Nikki shook her head. "Are you always so confident?"

An Important Message from the Publisher

Dear Reader,

Because you've chosen to read one of our fine novels, I'd like to say "thank you"! And, as a special way to say thank you, I'm offering to send you two more Kimani™ Romance novels and two surprise gifts—absolutely FREE! These books will keep it real with true-to-life African American characters that turn up the heat and sizzle with passion.

Please enjoy the free books and gifts with our compliments...

Glenda Howard
For Kimani Press

Peel off Seal and

Place Inside...

We'd like to send you two free books to introduce you to Kimani™ Romance books. These novels feature strong, sexy women, and African-American heroes that are charming, loving and true. Our authors fill each page with exceptional dialogue, exciting plot twists, and enough sizzling romance to keep you riveted until the very end!

KIMANI ROMANCE...LOVE'S ULTIMATE DESTINATION

Your two books have a combined cover price of $13.98, but are yours **FREE!**

We'll even send you two wonderful surprise gifts. You can't lose!

2 FREE BONUS GIFTS!

We'll send you two wonderful surprise gifts, (worth about $10) absolutely *FREE.* Just for giving KIMANI™ ROMANCE books a try! Don't miss out—*MAIL THE REPLY CARD TODAY!*

Visit us online at www.ReaderService.com

BUSINESS REPLY MAIL

FIRST-CLASS MAIL   PERMIT NO. 717   BUFFALO, NY

POSTAGE WILL BE PAID BY ADDRESSEE

THE READER SERVICE
PO BOX 1867
BUFFALO NY 14240-9952

NO POSTAGE
NECESSARY
IF MAILED
IN THE
UNITED STATES

▼ If offer card is missing write to: The Reader Service, P.O. Box 1867, Buffalo, NY 14240-1867 or visit www.ReaderService.com ▼

"Pretty much." He reached over and pushed back her hair.

Nikki shivered, but she didn't think that it had anything to do with the cold. Their eyes locked and that same electrical current came roaring back. For so long, she had stared at pictures of this man. They didn't hold a candle to the real thing.

"Do I make you nervous?"

"Who said I was nervous? I'm not nervous."

A low laugh rumbled through his chest. "Liar."

She thrust her chin up. "Am not."

"So it doesn't bother you when I do this?" His large but incredibly soft hands moved from her hair to her cold cheek where he seem to content himself with caressing for a long moment.

Nikki shivered. "No."

Hylan laughed again. "Why do you fascinate me so much?"

Don't fall for this, a tiny voice warned her. *The man is used to women falling at his feet.*

"When we kiss," he whispered, staring at her mouth. "I've never felt anything like it before."

Don't believe him. This is what he does. Stay tough. Hang in there. But it was hard not to believe him, because she had been feeling the same way. Her head wanted to believe it was just a figment of her imagination, but her heart wasn't buying it. There was definitely something happening between them and it was more powerful than anything she'd ever known.

When the moment was right for him to lean in and kiss her, he instead lowered his hand and pulled away.

"Sorry. I don't know what's gotten into me," he said. "One minute I want to throttle you and the next minute I want to make love to you."

Nikki's heart quickened at his confession. *He wants to make love to me.* The very idea tickled and thrilled her. Mainly because she suspected that making love to him would last a helluva lot longer than a couple of minutes. In fact, she was willing to bet everything she had, granted it wasn't much, that Hylan could do things to her body that she'd only read about in books.

"I bet you have this effect on a lot of guys," he guessed. "Men are always suckers for a damsel in distress."

She cocked her head as her eyes narrowed suspiciously. "Is that why you didn't tell everybody I'm a fraud? You think I'm a damsel in distress?"

"You are, aren't you?"

Nikki wanted to deny it, but this was one lie she couldn't get off the tip of her tongue so she cheated a bit. "Maybe."

Seeing her pride return in the stubborn set of her jaw, Hylan added, "I also did it because I like you."

She glanced at him from the corner of her eyes. "Really?"

He leaned closer. "I already told you that you fascinate me." His hand lifted and caressed her chin. "And I would be lying now if I said that I didn't want to kiss you again."

Nikki's heart leapt so high, she nearly choked on it. And when his head started descending, her stomach muscles flopped so loud, she was sure that people in

China heard them. When his lips were just inches away from hers, he stopped and gazed into her eyes.

"May I?"

No way could she talk with her heart in her throat, so she just nodded her head and waited for the fireworks. She didn't have to wait long.

Chapter 10

Nikki hadn't intended to make love to Hylan. It sort of just happened.

One moment she was sitting on the desk, moaning and quivering as his tongue explored her mouth and then the next moment that damn towel fell open. At least that's what she thinks happened. She wasn't too sure since her head grew hazy and her thoughts slowed. When Hylan's soft lips pulled away and he glanced down at her full breasts and erect nipples, his dark eyes sparkled with undeniable desire.

"Damn. You're so beautiful," he groaned, cupping her firm D-cups and giving them a gentle squeeze.

She moaned and closed her eyes.

"Your skin is so soft," he said, sounding fascinated.

He stroked her breasts a few times before his fingers zeroed in on pinching her hard nipples.

"Ooh." Her head fell back, exposing her long neck.

Hylan recognized an invitation when he saw one and leaned down to plant kisses on the line of her jaw all the way down to her sensitive collarbone. Kissing her was like finding the golden ticket to the chocolate factory. She tasted that damn sweet. What he really longed for was the taste of her caramel-tipped nipples. So much so that his stomach growled with hunger pangs.

Nikki was lost in the magic that Hylan was creating. As far as that little pesky voice in the back of her head, she'd gagged it and locked it in the deep recesses of her mind. All she wanted was for Hylan to keep doing what he was doing. She'd think about the consequences later. She sighed when Hylan's lips moved away from her neck then started to dip down toward the center of her body.

He was already the best she'd ever had because she'd never been with a man who'd even bothered with foreplay. Mindlessly, she ran her hand through his short cropped hair and then down his steely shoulders and then onto the hard planes of his back. Lord, he had an incredible body.

What she was feeling was nothing compared to the pleasure she felt when his mouth latched on to her cold nipples. Just the difference between his warm mouth and her cold nipple was enough to intensify the dull ache between her legs. In fact, her entire body had started to warm up. Maybe they weren't going to freeze to death down here after all.

Hylan sucked, licked and polished Nikki's perky nipples like a full-time job—and he didn't mind putting in some overtime. Then wanting to get more comfortable, he took her towel and placed it flat across the old desk and then eased her down. Lying down, she looked like an artist's masterpiece. No doubt about it, she was definitely someone that he wanted to take his time with, and given their current situation, they had nothing but time on their hands. He started to climb up on the desk with her, when she held out a hand to stop him.

"Take yours off," she whispered.

Hylan glanced down and knew that she was referring to his towel. "You do it." Instantly, her lips quirked up with a mischievous smile, but he waited patiently as she slowly lifted a hand and then slipped it down the front of his towel. The heavy terry-cloth tented higher. Still, he waited, watching her face for a reaction when she finally saw *all* of him.

He wasn't disappointed.

Nikki gave the towel a quick tug and it fell from his tapered hips easily. As creative and inventive as her imagination could get, it failed to do Hylan Dawson's powerful physique justice. His smooth, thick and long cock needed to be in a museum or something. Its full mushroom head with its cute indentation at the top practically begged to be touched and caressed and she didn't want to disappoint the handsome fella.

At the first touch of her fingers, Hylan sucked in a breath that made his dick jump in her hands. But when her hands wrapped around his thick shaft and began to slide up and down, his body experienced its own spike in temperature. He moved closer to the desk, giving her room and an opportunity to glide her hand all the way down to the base of his cock and then up around his purpling head.

When his gaze returned to her face, he loved the way she seemed fascinated by what she was doing. At that moment, he knew he had to have her—more than he needed air to breathe. The look of raw desire sparkling in her eyes as well, let him know he *would* have her.

"You have the prettiest dick I've ever seen," she whispered.

He laughed, his cock jumping in her hand as he did so. "I don't think I've ever heard Junior described as pretty before."

"Junior?"

Hylan carefully climbed up on the desk like a prowling panther. "I had to name him something. After all, he has a mind of his own." He kissed her softly.

"Really?" she asked, fighting back a giggle.

"Um-hmm." His head sank lower so he could nibble on her right earlobe.

She released her hold and in return his heavy cock smacked against her flat stomach. "Oh God," she quivered and trembled. How many times had she sat looking at his pictures, wondering what it would be like to make love to him? Probably too many to count. A man with his reputation, it was only natural for a woman's curiosity to be piqued.

And now that she stood at the brink of doing something that she'd only dreamed of, that flopping in her belly stopped and what felt like a million butterflies started fluttering in perfect unison. Was it possible to have stage fright before sex? With so little experience, what if he was disappointed in her performance? That scary thought raced through her mind for a second but in the next, Hylan's mouth returned to her breasts and her head, once again, emptied of all thoughts.

In no time at all, the burgeoning lovers turned that ice-box of a basement into a raging inferno. Nikki's limbs felt as though they were melting—but in a good way, in fact, in the best way possible. His mouth and hands weren't just kissing her, they were worshipping her. And the lower his head went, the more butterflies broke from their cocoons.

"Spread your legs for me, baby." He kissed her just above the door of her femininity and then watched as she opened herself up before his greedy eyes.

With lust-filled eyes, she watched a broad smile slide across his lips. Nikki's heart skipped a beat at his obvious approval and waited with bated breath to see what he would do next. She thought that he would just get to the nitty-gritty and dive in, but he surprised her by raining more kisses on her thighs and behind her knees. Then, she felt the feathery touch of his index finger glide along the lips of her pussy. She was wet before, but she was practically drenched now.

The kissing continued as he slowly dipped his finger in to test the waters. It sailed inside with a silky squish and then flickered at the base of her clit.

"Oh my God," she panted as her eyes damn near rolled to the back of her head.

"You like that, hmm?" Hylan asked, his mouth creeping so close she could feel his breath warming the corner of her thigh. When she didn't answer, mainly because she couldn't, he slipped in a second finger.

Nikki's hips came up off the desk, but that only helped his fingers sink deeper.

"How about that?" he asked. "Is that better?"

"O-oh God, yes." She tried to lower her hips, but for each stroke of his fingers, they came back up and he would go even deeper. It was a wonderful roller coaster ride that kept her dizzy. Again, that was nothing compared to when Hylan's mouth finally settled over her pink clit. "Aw," she moaned. Tears surfaced and leaked out of the corners of her eyes as she shuddered in delight. His tongue made lazy figure eights against her clit, while his fingers continued their deep stroking.

Approaching delirium, Nikki tossed her head from side to side. Her hips surged and rotated while her breathing thinned to the point that she was either coming or about to go into cardiac arrest.

Hylan kept lapping her up as her body's honey trickled against his tongue. The woman just kept on getting sweeter and he knew that at any moment he was going to be suffering from a sugar high. He removed his hand and stiffened his tongue to hit the lining of her pussy.

Nikki's entire body vibrated. Her heart was seconds from pounding its way out of her chest and a sudden white light appeared from behind her closed eyelids. Whatever self-control she'd held onto was tossed out the window when Hylan's tongue hit the right spot at the right time. She cried out his name as her legs collapsed and her knees locked behind his head.

And yet, Hylan's tongue refused to relent. She inched up the desk and tried to push his head away, but with her locked knees, her efforts were rendered useless.

"I—I can't breathe," she gasped, but even that declaration failed to get her any mercy. A second orgasm started building at the base of her clit and before she could prepare herself Hylan hit the detonation button and her body gushed more honey than he knew what to do with.

Satisfied that she was primed and ready, Hylan reached behind his head and pulled her legs open. One glance at the table, he knew that there was really only one position that was going to work best for them. He climbed up her body and pressed a kiss against her lips so he could share her rich taste. "I want you to ride me, baby. You think you can do that?"

Hell yeah. Of course if he said that he wanted her to swing from the moon, she would have agreed to that, too.

He effortlessly shifted their bodies so that he laid back on the damp towel and she lay on top of him. When she pushed herself up so she could straddle him, the fear of not being experienced enough came raging back. Up until now, she had only had sex in the missionary position. But how hard could this be? She looked down and tried to decide whether she should plant her feet on either side of him or on her knees.

"Is there something wrong?" he asked.

Nikki's face heated with embarrassment. "No.

I—um…" She fumbled, deciding to put her feet down.

"You've done this before, haven't you? You're not a virgin…are you?"

"No," she snapped, close to tears. "It's just that I've never…"

Hylan sat up and delivered another kiss against her trembling lips. "Shh. It's okay." He reached down and helped position her knees on the hardwood desk while her lips parted, inviting his tongue.

She quivered when his tongue licked the inside of her cheek. While he distracted her with his erotic kiss, his hand reached in between their bodies and shifted his steel-like erection into her silky opening. Her body's wet lips parted easily, accommodating the thick mushroom head of his cock.

"Hold on to me," he whispered.

Nikki complied by gripping his shoulders and then fervently prayed that she would be able to take in all of him.

"Roll your hips for me, baby," he whispered raggedly.

Again, she followed orders and started rotating her hips and could feel his thick shaft slowly ease into her tight walls inch by glorious inch. There was so much of him that Nikki started to tense up, which only tightened her wall.

Hylan hissed as his face contorted with pleasure. She was as tight as a drum and it was making his toes curl. "I need you to relax, baby. Relax."

She tried, but was having a hard time of it. There

was no way she was going to be able to fit him all the way in. No way.

Realizing that he needed to loosen her up or come prematurely, Hylan slipped his other hand in between them and started rubbing her clit with the pad of his thumb. He smiled when he heard her small gasp, but more importantly, he felt her when her muscles loosened and more honey lubricated her inner walls. "Ah. That's it, baby," he praised. After a few more strokes to her clit, he managed to impale her with his full length.

Nikki's head was lost in the clouds. She was vaguely aware of his hands settling on her hips and helping her make small bounces up and down on his cock. That was about it. She was too consumed by a bliss that she could never put into words. One thing she knew for sure, she never wanted it to end.

Hylan got off watching Nikki's enraptured face as much as the feel of her body gliding up and down him. He thought that she was beautiful before, but now she had a glow about her that was positively breathtaking. His hands slid up from her waist back up to her full breasts, where he squeezed and pinched her hard nipples. *Damn. This woman could get a brotha caught up.*

Her muscles tightened again. His hands fell back to her hips as he clamped his jaw tight. When he felt it again, he knew what was happening. "Are you ready to come, baby?"

Her answer was a helpless whimper as her fingers dug into his shoulders.

He reached up again, this time pulling her close so

that her jiggling breasts rocked against his chest and his face buried in her damp hair. "You coming, baby?" he asked, because he was cruising toward that cliff himself. "Tell me, baby. I don't want to come without you."

She whimpered and tightened again.

Hylan's hips picked up speed. His low, deep moans blended with her whimpering sighs to make their own unique music. Soon after, he knew the evitable was approaching. "Come with me, baby," he pleaded.

Nikki's lips found his just as they took that final leap and cried out into the stratosphere. They soared for so high and so long, it truly felt as if they were never going to come back down. One thing for sure, if and when they did, nothing would ever be the same between them.

Chapter 11

Hours later, Nikki's eyes fluttered open. At first she was confused to find herself curled into the crook of a man's arms. Let's face it, it didn't happen often. When she inhaled the man's now-familiar scent and took note of the delicious ache between her thighs, everything came back to her in vibrant color and put a big ole smile on her face.

She slowly and gently tried to lift her head so she could get a better look at her new lover. It wasn't easy because Hylan had completely encased her in his arms as if he was a human blanket. For the most part, it worked. She wasn't the slightest bit cold. But how long had they been down there? It was impossible to tell, with there being no windows and all. Of course the more important question was how long *would* they be down there. Maybe they would be down there long enough to have sex again.

She definitely wouldn't mind that. Hell, until Hylan, she thought sex was overrated when the truth was, she'd been missing out. Nikki then wondered if he would object if she woke him up for another go-round. Then again, she'd never heard of a man turning down sex before. But how should she go about doing it—tap him on the shoulder and ask him politely? Maybe just roll him back onto his back and hop on top of him. She sort of liked riding on top.

"I take it that all the squirming you're doing means that you're awake?" Hylan said, his chin bumping against the top of her head.

"Sorry. Did I wake you?" she asked, timidly.

"No." His arms tightened around her. "I've been awake for a few minutes...thinking."

Hearing the heavy note in his voice, Nikki suspected his *thinking* wasn't a good sign. But as the silence stretched between them, she felt compelled to ask, "What were you thinking about?"

"Us," he stated simply.

She knew it. Nikki closed her eyes and cursed herself for giving into him so easily. She *knew* that he was the type to just hit it and quit it and she screwed him anyway. Why was she always making such stupid mistakes?

Nikki pushed at Hylan's arms. "Let me up."

"Why? What's wrong?"

Tears stung Nikki's eyes as she pushed again. "I said, let me up!"

Hylan finally relented and unfolded his arms. "You're angry," he said.

"I am not," she lied, climbing off the desk and fighting back tears.

"What is it with you? Why can't you just be *honest* with me?" he thundered. "If I've done something to upset you, then just say so."

Nikki snatched her towel and tilted her chin while she covered her nude body.

Hylan huffed out an exasperated breath. "I must be out of my mind, thinking that I wanted to try to get to know you better. To do that would require *honest* communication."

"It's not you, okay?" She tossed up her hands, exasperated. "It's me. It's *always* me." Nikki drew in a deep breath, but as she exhaled her body trembled. "What happened here...between us...was a mistake," she finally choked out.

"Oh really?" Hylan sat up. Unashamed of his body, he made no attempt to cover up.

"C'mon." She shook her head. "Let's be real. We hardly even know each other."

"Apparently, that didn't stop us from getting married."

"Ha-ha. Now look who's being a comedian."

"Guilty," he said. "I'm trying to lighten the mood here. Forgive me. But I just don't know when everything turned so serious between us."

"That's just it," she charged, looking to meet his confused gaze. "You don't take any relationship seriously. You're a certified playa, womanizer, philanderer, gigolo—"

"Ah, ah, ah. Gigolo implies that I've had sex for money and I've *never* gone down that slippery slope."

"See. You can't even be serious about this," she said, tossing up her hands. The basement's chill returned and started to seep into her bones. She shivered and hugged herself.

"Will you just come back over here and let me warm you up?"

"No, thank you. I know the kind of warming up you have in mind."

Irritation tightened Hylan's jaw. "I don't recall you complaining earlier."

"That's because I couldn't think straight."

"And now you are?" he asked.

Hell no! "Yes," she lied again. "And I think getting involved with you would be a huge mistake."

"Again, you can't get involved with me, but you can tell anyone who'll stand still that we're married?"

Nikki stomped her foot against the concrete. "Will you stop bringing that up?"

"Excuuuse me. Well, it is the big pink elephant in the room." He shook his head at this unbelievable conversation. "I mean, how am I to take that you don't mind pretending to be my wife, but you're suddenly repulsed by the idea of making love to me?"

"What? No. I didn't say that." She drew a deep breath and tried to figure her loopy thinking out. "I just meant that…"

"You just meant what?" he pressed.

Nikki forced her gaze back to his. "I just know that you and me…would never work out. You're the kind of guy that doesn't stick around." She watched him as he drew in a deep breath. "I know that my sleeping with you is just going to complicate matters. I'm already feeling things that…" she dropped her head back down.

Hylan knew where she was going, even though he didn't like it. And he knew that she was right. But it didn't stop him from wanting her. "Look," he started softly. "Maybe things are going a little fast between us but…I, in no way, think that what happened down here was a mistake."

"You don't?" Her surprise echoed clearly in her voice.

Hylan stood and walked over to her. "Of course not." He pulled her into his arms. "Trust me. If not now, I would've been plotting and strategizing to get you into my bed before you left here."

She stiffened. "So what? I'm just another notch on your bedpost, or better yet, your desk?"

Hylan huffed out a long exasperated breath. "Woman, will you stop? You're thinking too much. "There's nothing wrong with just living in the moment. Just enjoy whatever this is we're feeling while we feel it."

It sounded good, but Nikki wasn't sure what it was she was feeling. What part of it was fantasy and what part of it was real?

"You're doing it again."

She looked up with questioning eyes.

"You're thinking too much." His head descended and chanced stealing a kiss. His risk paid off when his lips brushed against hers. Just like all the other times before, his mind spun as if he'd taken a hit from some illegal drug.

Nikki's wall of resistance crumbled without much of a fight. What she was doing was dangerous—and yet, she couldn't stop herself. She loved his lips. They were soft and full and had a way of making her feel complete. He lifted his large masculine hands and massaged the back of her neck. Her heart started skipping again and all those wonderful butterflies began fluttering again.

Hylan scooped her up and carried her back over to the old wooden desk without ever breaking their kiss. He eased her back like he'd been playing this part for their entire lifetime.

A familiar heat rushed through Nikki. She needed him—right then and there. He ripped the towel from her body as if it offended him and then covered her body with his own. She shook uncontrollably as Hylan's mouth moved to light other fires across her body. In no time, she was anxious for their bodies to join. She remembered vividly how it felt to have him stroking deep within her. However, Hylan didn't seem to be in any rush. He let his mouth and hands perform their own brand of black magic, so much so that she could feel a fresh wave of tears slide from her eyes.

When he finally slid into the space between her legs, Nikki's curvy hips lifted in greeting and then met each thrust pound for pound.

"You feel so good," he praised, rocking smooth and steady.

Nikki wanted to answer but there were no words

to describe what he was doing to her. Besides, it took everything she had just to keep drawing oxygen into her body. But she tried to express in her eyes what her mouth failed to do. He smiled down at her as if her message had been received. More tears surfaced and rolled down the corners of her eyes, but he was right there to kiss them away.

"Does this feel like a mistake to you, baby?"

Nikki shook her head.

"Tell me, baby. Was this a mistake?"

"N-no."

His smile broadened and strokes quickened.

Then she felt it, that wonderful sensation that blossomed from the center of her body and then spread out until every atom in her body tingled and vibrated. Suddenly the blood rushing through her head sounded like a freight train. Her submissive whimpers and sighs morphed quickly into higher octaves of pleasure. Then his name burst from her lips in a final scream of ecstasy.

Hylan's lusty growl followed close behind. His body trembled and shook for a while as her inner muscles kept tightening and then released him during her aftershocks. When he finally collapsed down next to her, he gathered her close so he could cocoon her with his body heat.

"I don't ever want to hear you say that this was a mistake again," he whispered and pressed a kiss against her forehead.

Nikki smiled as her eyelids grew heavy. *It wasn't a mistake,* she recited in her head. *It wasn't a mistake.* Just before she drifted off to sleep, she almost believed it.

Chapter 12

"Well, Lord shut my mouth!"

Hylan and Nikki's eyes sprung open a second before their heads jerked up from the old wooden desk. A red-faced Mahina turned her back and fanned herself to give them time to collect themselves.

"My goodness. I guess I should have knocked."

Nikki and Hylan scrambled off the desk and grabbed their towels.

"Thank God you came over," Nikki panted in a squeaky high voice. "We didn't know how long we were going to be down here."

"Yeah," Hylan said, wrapping his towel snugly around his hips. "Looks like we really owe you one."

"Looks to me like you two found something to occupy your time."

He laughed. "We made do."

Nikki smacked him in the arm and gave him a glare that told him to behave.

Hylan continued laughing. "You know all this abuse I've been getting down here has got to stop."

She only rolled her eyes and marched toward the door. "Thanks again, Mahina." Nikki dipped her embarrassed head low as she passed by Mahina and headed toward the door.

"Yep. You're a life saver," he added. He was bold enough to give her a kiss on the cheek before exiting the basement.

"Lord. Lord. Lord," she said and shook her head.

Nikki raced up the basement stairs and had every intention of bounding up the main staircase as well, but then came to a screeching halt when she saw a foyer filled with people.

"I finally found them," Mahina shouted as she came up the stairs.

Hylan walked into the foyer behind Nikki and was equally stunned to see that they had company. "Aunt Addie," he said as he recognized the short, silver-haired woman in front of the pack.

A roomful of eyes widened and raked over Nikki and Hylan. Then there was a series of snickers before a full-blown explosion of laughter.

"Did we catch you two at a bad time?" Addie asked, pushing her thin, wire-rimmed glasses up the bridge of her nose.

"What are you all doing here?" Hylan asked.

Nikki took a few steps back and hid behind Hylan's large frame.

Aunt Addie's face scrunched up into a frown. "Well, word got to me that you've been here on this island for the past 48 hours and didn't have the decency to come by and see me."

A few uncles and cousins bobbed their heads in agreement.

"It's bad enough that you'd run off and got married without inviting a single family member to the wedding. Not that we don't just adore Nikki," she hastily added. "I gotta hand it to you for picking out such an angel. Why all the work she does down at the church has endeared her to a lot folks around here."

Hylan glanced back at his *wife*. "Yeah. It seems her good works have no ending."

"Thanks, Aunt Addie," Nikki chirped from behind Hylan's muscled forearm.

"Why none of us would've ever believed that you would pick out such a nice, stable woman with her head screwed on after watching you parade a dozen hoochie mommas around here that probably didn't know the difference between a pot and a skillet."

Hylan laughed at his *stable wife*. "Sorry about that. I didn't know that the family was on hoochie momma watch."

"Well," Aunt Addie said, straightening her hunched shoulders the best she could. "I know your momma would be proud."

Hylan's gaze fell away at the mention of his mother, but a second later he flashed a smile. "I apologize,

Aunt Addie. I wasn't trying to avoid you." He stepped forward as if he was going to give the woman a hug, but Nikki quickly wrapped an arm around his waist to keep him just where he was, shielding her from view— specifically from Hylan's Uncle Edrian. No doubt back in his heyday, his uncle was as much a playboy as his nephew, but clearly he hadn't gotten the memo that his shenanigans had put him solidly in the "dirty old man" column.

Hylan picked up on the hint and stayed put. "It's just that it's been a little crazy around here since I got back. You know, the storm and the roads being closed."

"Uh-huh," Aunt Addie said, unimpressed with the flimsy excuse.

Momma Mahina finally rode into the rescue. "How about we all go into the kitchen and give these two some time to get dressed?"

Nikki sighed in relief, seeing how they all seemed content to just let her and Hylan stand there in towels while they conducted their family reunion. "Thank you, Mahina."

"Since you cooked breakfast for Lathan and me yesterday, I'll return the favor," Mahina said, shuffling off.

"Well, I can help you with that," Addie said. "We can just make a big buffet for everyone."

That announcement solicited a few more volunteers to help.

"This isn't over, young man," Aunt Addie said, waving her finger. "You've got a lot of explaining to do." Again her gaze shifted to Nikki. "But I'm glad you came home. You have a helluva woman right there."

Nikki groaned as the weight of her lies grew heavier.

"You don't have to tell me that," Hylan said, turning and swinging his arm around his wife. "She's the salt of the earth." He gave her a hard squeeze and watched her struggle not to cry out.

Hylan and Nikki watched the herd of people shuffle toward the kitchen. When they were alone, his arm fell from her shoulders.

"I'm so sorry," Nikki said, feebly.

His brows arched upward. "Really?" He dipped his finger down the front of her towel and peeked down. "'Cuz I can think of a few ways you can repay me."

Playfully, she smacked his hand away. "Again? So soon? You're kidding me."

"We both have to the hit the showers again anyway."

Nikki giggled at the devilish grin that slithered across his full lips.

"My God. You're insatiable."

"Hmm. I seem to recall you telling me that on our wedding night."

Her expression twisted in confusion.

"What?" he asked, looking insulted. "You're not the only one with a creative imagination in this family."

Nikki laughed and then emitted a startled cry when he bent down and scooped her up in his arms and carried her up the stairs.

* * *

A week later, the roads were all clear, the skies were blue and Nicole Jamison was still masquerading as Hylan Dawson's wife. It probably had a lot to do with the fact that the new lovers simply couldn't get enough of each other. Both knew that continuing the lie was wrong, but things had gotten so complicated that neither could see a way out without causing a lot of hurt and pain. So for the time being there was just an unspoken understanding that they were in this thing together. When Hylan left to return to Atlanta, she would leave too, only she would be heading home to New York. Down the road when Hylan returned to the island he'd simply say that things hadn't worked out and that they'd divorced. Problem solved.

Meanwhile, Hylan had to admit that he was actually having the vacation of a lifetime. For the first time in his life, he was with a woman who actually enjoyed the physical activities that the island had to offer. His and Nikki's days were filled with hiking, swimming, scuba diving, Jet Skiing and everything else in between.

In the past, his dates were of the high-maintenance variety who rarely did anything other than lie on the beach, sip colorful drinks and hit the sack. But Nikki, he discovered, had a fierce competitive side. Whether it was swimming, volley ball or Jet Ski racing, the woman gave a hundred and ten percent.

She always lost.

But it wasn't for lack of trying.

Nikki also had a few more talents—she was an excellent dancer and could play the piano, guitar and the ukulele. *Who plays the ukulele?* Then Nikki told him about the endless lessons she had coerced her parents into enrolling her in. She never finished any of them, but she managed to learn enough to get by.

While she seemed ashamed for never having finished any of these pursuits, Hylan had to admit that he was impressed that she even tried. "How do you know whether you'll truly like something unless you try?"

"I never really thought about it like that," she admitted, over dinner at the Rainforest Hideaway.

"That's called living in the moment," he said, winking. "Besides, the best time to do all that stuff is when you're a kid."

She laughed and shook her head. "I wish my father would've seen it that way."

Hylan was starting not to like her father. Clearly, her father's disapproval weighed heavily on Nikki.

"He always said that I lacked focus and discipline." She cracked open a crab leg and pulled out the succulent meat with her fingers.

"And what do you think?" he asked, reaching for his beer.

Nikki shrugged. "I don't know. Maybe he's right."

"I don't think so."

Her head came up. "You don't?"

"Nope." He smiled. "It's your life. No one can decide what's best for you other than you. So what, you've fallen on your ass a few times. You're supposed to."

"I am?"

Hylan bobbed his head and loved seeing a new light flicker in her eyes. "How else are you going to learn what not to do next time? All the great successes have fallen on their asses at one time or another. The secret has always been getting back up."

Nikki thrust out her chin, her heart inspired by Hylan's words. "You know what? I think I have a play I need to finish."

"That's my girl."

Nikki wasted no time pounding away on the keyboard. With a newfound energy and Hylan's moral support, her fingers could barely keep up with the words spilling out of her head. Hylan slid easily into the role of cooking her breakfast, lunch and dinner and serving it up to her on a tray at her desk. When she finally started printing pages, he was honored that she wanted him to read it and give her some honest feedback.

"Are you sure?" he asked, worried that her newfound confidence was too fragile to accept honest criticism.

"Yes, yes. I'm sure." She rushed to pull up a chair for him. "Now sit down."

He quickly plopped down and took a look at the freshly printed pages. But after a few seconds, he looked into Nikki's eager eyes. "Are you just going to sit there and watch me read?"

"Yeah. Why?"

He quirked a smile. "It might be a little distracting don't you think?"

Nikki's smile curled upside down. "I just want to make sure that you laugh in the right spots."

He leveled her with a look that said, "Are you for real?"

"All right. All right. I'll turn around." She huffed, crossed her arms and swiveled her chair around. "Better?"

Hylan laughed. "Better." He eased back in his chair and immediately began to read. Within seconds, he was laughing.

Nikki twisted her chair around. "You laughed. Which part did you think was funny?"

Hylan glanced back and twirled his finger, indicating for her to turn back around.

"But—"

"No buts. Turn around. I can't read with you watching me."

"You know what? I'll just go downstairs and wait until you're finished."

He shrugged. "Okay."

She stood there as if she'd expected him to tell her to stay. When that didn't happen, she had no choice but to leave. Still holding out hope, she poked out her bottom lip and dragged her feet.

Hylan just snickered and shook his head at her pitiful performance. "Um—"

"Yes?" Nikki pivoted with hope gleaming in her eyes.

"Make sure you close the door behind you," he said. "I want to make sure I give this my full attention."

She stood there, blinking at him.

"Thanks," he added, smiling. Nikki turned back toward the door, but he caught how her bottom lip poked out even farther. When she finally reached the door and started to close it, he gave her a quick little wave.

Nikki closed the door, but then pressed her ear against it to check whether she could hear anything. Seconds later, she heard Hylan's laughter rumble through the door. She smiled to herself and then sat down on the floor and continued to listen.

An hour later, Hylan turned the last page of Nikki's script and roared at the final scene. He could honestly say that it was the best thing he'd read in some time. The woman was indeed talented. Surely with the right backing, the play actually had a reasonable chance of being a success—as long as she didn't act in it. He immediately wondered if he could talk a few of the other Kappa brothers into investing in the production.

He reached into his pants pockets and retrieved his cell phone. He punched in Taariq's number and held the phone, waiting for a connection. It came as no surprise when he reached Taariq's voice mail. "Yo, T, it's me. Give me a call out at my vacay when you get this message. Thanks." He hung up and then called out to Nikki. "You can come in now," he said, knowing full well that she'd planted herself outside the door.

Sure enough, Nikki came rushing into the room. "So did you like it? You can tell me. I can take it."

Hylan laughed. "You know full well that I liked it. I'm sure you heard me laughing through the door."

Nikki jumped and danced around like a football player who had just crossed the goal line. And before he knew it, she was leaping into his arms and smothering him with kisses.

Chapter 13

Hylan knew just how to celebrate Nikki completing her play. He packed them a good lunch and then headed out onto one of the estate's many hidden trails. The hiking adventure wasn't for the faint of heart. The rough terrain could be a challenge for even the most experienced hikers. At this point, Hylan knew that Nikki could, in fact, keep up.

And he was right.

Glancing back over his shoulder, he caught glimpses of the broad smile on Nikki's face as she drank in the trail's unfolding beauty. He couldn't imagine anyone not being swept away by the rain forest's gigantic ferns, exotic birds and gorgeous flowers with colors that spanned the rainbow. This had to be what the Garden of Eden looked like.

"I don't think I've been on this trail before."

"I'm not surprised. It's one of my secret treasures."

"It's beautiful out here," Nikki said in awe.

"You haven't seen nothin' yet." He reached back for her hand and then braided their fingers so that they could walk the remaining distance together. After rounding a couple more bends, there was the unmistakable sound of rushing water.

Nikki squeezed his hand. "A waterfall?"

"I hope you don't mind taking a swim?"

Her brows shot up in amusement. "But we didn't pack any swimsuits."

"C'mon now. You should know better than that." He winked.

A delicious thrill skipped down Nikki's spine and her lips blossomed into a beautiful smile. "I'll race you." Before he could respond, she dropped his hand and took off running up the trail.

"Cheater!" Hylan sped after and, despite her long legs, caught up to her just before she made it to the clearing.

Nikki laughed and tried to wiggle free to complete the race but he locked a muscled arm around her waist and anchored her in place. "Let me go."

"No. No," he said, pulling her close. "I don't want you to ruin the surprise. I want to see the look on your face when I show you my private spot." He kissed her.

"Uh-huh." She broke the kiss to roll her eyes skeptically. "And just how many women have seen this private spot?"

He shook his head. "I've never brought anyone else here."

"Yeah, right." She playfully pushed at his chest, not buying that line at all.

"I'm being serious," he insisted. "This is my own private spot." He glanced around. "I come up here to think and relax. Plus, you're the only woman I know who would hike that trail to get up here."

"Ah. So it's not that you didn't *want* to bring anyone else up here."

He just laughed at her tactics. "No. You're the first person I've wanted to bring."

Biting her bottom lip, Nikki narrowed her eyes and studied him. "I think you might be telling the truth."

"Cross my heart." He kissed her again. "Hope to die."

Nikki slid her arms around his neck and deepened their kiss. Each time their mouths touched it was as powerful as the first time. When Hylan pulled back, she moaned with disappointment. Tasting him never lasted long enough.

"Are you ready to go see my private paradise?"

"Absolutely." She eased under the crook of his arm and wrapped hers around his waist as he led her around the last bend. At the first sight of the waterfall, Nikki felt her entire body light up. The lush vegetation and wild and exotic flowers created a beautiful grotto with a large, natural rock pool.

"Do you like it?" he asked.

"I think I've died and gone to heaven," she said, not

wanting to take her eyes from the magnificent natural sight.

"Well, I know I have." He pressed a kiss against her temple and declared, "The last one in naked is a rotten egg." He dropped his arms and raced toward the waterfall while stripping his shirt over his head.

"Cheater!" Nikki shouted, taking off after him and fumbling with her own clothes.

No surprise that Hylan was the first to cannonball into the air and hit the warm spring with a resounding splash! A second later, he resurfaced pumping his fist into the air. "Yeah! Victory!"

Unfazed by her second-place finish, Nikki stripped out of the last of her clothes and leaped in with a gleeful, "Whee!"

Hylan laughed at her antics and quickly encircled her when she bobbed back up to the surface. "You, my beautiful darling, are what I like to call a loser!"

"Am not!" Nikki slapped the water, causing it to spray his face.

"See what I mean?" He reached out to grab her but she leaned out of reach. "Whatcha grabbin' at, huh?"

Hylan lunged and missed again. "Come back here, you."

"Why?" she taunted. "What could you possibly want with a loser like me?"

"Trust me. I can think of a few things." He dove under the water.

Nikki turned and swam like hell toward the grotto. Just as she was maneuvering around the powerful waterfall, Hylan caught hold of her foot. However, she was a slippery devil and managed to make it to the cave beyond. Climbing out, she started to turn and pump her fist into the air for having successfully gotten away, but something caught her attention within the cave. "There's something in here," she said.

A smiling Hylan came out of the water behind her. "Then let's go check out what it is."

"Are you crazy? I'm not going in there. It's dark."

He eased his arms around her and pulled her wet, naked body against him. "Don't worry, baby. I've got you."

Nikki smiled when her butt brushed against his erection. "What are you up to?" she asked suspiciously.

"I thought that would be obvious." Hylan kept one arm locked around her waist and then slid his free hand down and in between her thighs.

Reflexively, she widened her stance to give him more room.

"Thank you, baby," he whispered and then dipped his large fingers in between the wet folds of her pussy. "Mmm. Nice." He skimmed his mouth down her neck.

She couldn't have agreed more and wiggled back against his growing cock. "What did you put in the cave?" she asked.

"Don't worry. You'll see in a few minutes. Let me just finish playing with my friend here." He eased below the bottom of her clit and stirred his finger around. "Look at you. You're already wet." He added a second finger and then relished the sound of her soft sighs. He worked her just enough to get her hot and then pulled out.

Nikki's lashes fluttered upward while her eyes flickered with disappointment.

Hylan smacked her on the ass. "C'mon. You want to see what's in here or not?"

"It can wait," she whined, grabbing his hand and pressing it back between her legs.

Hylan laughed. "It looks like somebody's greedy."

"Just a little." She wiggled some more, but only received another smack on the ass. "Everything in due time, sweetheart. Now come on."

Pushing out her bottom lip, Nikki allowed him to lead her back to the dark cave. It turned out that they didn't have to venture too far in when he turned on a battery-operating camp light that was propped up against the rock wall. Instantly the small cave lit up and revealed a vibrant mural that stretched around the entire wall.

"Oh my God, it's beautiful."

"You like it?" His voice perked up.

"Like it?" Her gaze slowly roamed over the abstract piece. "How can I not? It's amazing."

"Thanks."

She finally whipped her head toward him. "*You* painted this?"

Hylan's handsome face darkened with embarrassed modesty. "I tell myself that I'm not really this artsy fartsy kind of guy, but this kind of stuff soothes me. Especially with the waterfall and all."

"Artsy fartsy?" She laughed and shivered.

"Oh, are you cold?" He rushed over to one corner where there were a few long trunks stored. He opened one and pulled out two long beach towels.

"Don't tell me you live out here."

"No. I'm just the kind of guy who believes in always being prepared." He handed her one of the towels. "Besides, I'd planned yesterday to bring you out here." He nodded toward the opposite wall.

As she draped the towel around her body, she turned toward a nice cozy corner with a small table and picnic basket. Next to it lay a bed, complete with black sheets and covered with the petals of the various flowers they'd seen during their trek. "Oh, Hylan." She stepped forward. "When did you have time to do all of this?"

He eased back up behind her. "Yesterday, while you were writing." He pulled her hair up and started seducing her neck again. "Do you like it?" His peeled open the towel.

"Mmm. You know I do." She leaned her head back, hoping his mouth would hit the side of her neck, which seemed to be one of her G-spots. The cave was just so exotic and extraordinarily different than any date she had been on that she had to give him extra brownie points for thinking of it.

"Are you hungry?" he asked, sliding his hands under her breasts. He gave them a good squeeze and a light jiggle.

"Mmm-hmm. But not for food." She turned in his arms and kissed him with a passion and vigor that even surprised her. She gave herself a mental high-five when she heard *him* moan. That small victory had her lowering her arms and gliding her hand from his broad neck down his muscled chest. There her fingers made soft laps around his nipples.

Hylan's dick sprung up so high and hard that it breached the thick lips of her pussy and bumped up against her clit with no help from its owner. Nikki could easily widen her stance again and offer Junior a nice warm place to get comfortable, but she was ready to do something she'd been thinking about since that fateful night in the basement.

"C'mere, baby." She backed out of his arms and took him by the hand and led him to the flower bed.

Hylan had always known when to shut up and follow orders. As she led him to the air mattress bed, he took the moment to drink in every detail from her smiling face to her clear painted toenails. She was a natural beauty through and through. How in the hell did he get so lucky?

Nikki stepped on the bed and immediately sank to her knees.

Hylan was a bit surprised. He'd pegged her as a girl who didn't perform oral sex and something about the way her hand trembled slightly confirmed that. "Baby you don't have to," he said, reaching to pull her up.

"No. I want to," she insisted, wrapping her hand around his thick cock. Immediately, a few drops of pre-cum dripped from the bulbous head. Nikki stared at it for a few seconds while she continued to stroke him.

Hylan couldn't decided if she was either scared or in a trance, but he was still loving the feel of her silky hands work their magic. "Baby, I mean it. You don't…"

That was all he got out, before Nikki flicked her tongue against the head of his dick. He gasped as stars exploded behind his eyes. Before he could catch his breath, her pink tongue returned and snaked up and around his cock with such delicious efficiency that he had to clench his ass muscles to prevent him from shooting off before he was out of the starting gate.

Nikki didn't make it any easier for him. Once she got a good taste of his sweet candy cane, she dropped her jaw open and tried her best to swallow him whole. Of course, she didn't come anywhere close, but she certainly did enough to send his ass to the moon. She slurped, popped her cheek and then went back down again.

"Oh, damn, baby." Hylan threaded his large hands through her hair. "You're a damn natural at this."

The compliment boosted Nikki's confidence and gave her the swag to increase the suction and make sure her tongue caressed every protruding vein along the way.

Mercury, Venus, Mars—Hylan was seeing the entire solar system in his head while simultaneously moaning and hissing. But then she threw another curve into his game by poppin' her mouth off his cock and then running that wonderful tongue up and around his heavy balls.

"Damn. Damn. Damn," he couldn't stop repeating the word. Then, as a last ditch effort to save himself, he stepped back and swung his cock away from her greedy mouth. "I'm gonna hand it to you, ma. You got skills. But I think I'm a little hungry myself."

"But I wasn't finished," Nikki pouted. She was just getting pretty good.

Hylan moved back toward the bed. "Trust that your man has a solution for that."

My man? Just the thought of him being *her* man thrilled her. Pretending to be married to him had been one thing, but this new reality—or possibility—was something totally different.

Next thing she knew she was laying back, spread-eagle with Hylan's talented tongue licking the face of her strawberry-color clit as if it was manna from heaven and pumping his fingers in and out until she could feel her liquid candy gush out of her. Nikki was putting in work, too. Her arms were wrapped around his waist while his cock was planted back into her mouth for her first 69. The way things were going, and feeling, it definitely wasn't going to be her last.

Then her hips started moving when that wonderful tingling sensation started pulsing through her. She wanted to come and come hard. The way Hylan's tongue was slapping the hell out of her G-spot there was a one hundred percent chance that she was going to get her wish. Equally determined to send his ass to another galaxy, Nikki pushed his cock to the side of her mouth and redoubled her sucking motion.

Hylan's mouth near popped off the head of her clit at the feel of her jaw breaking his cock. His nut started to rise up and he knew that it was on then. Both were competing to make the other come first.

He tried to control his breathing. That didn't work.

He tried curling his toes. That didn't work either.

He clenched his ass cheeks. And that wasn't working either.

He was about to come. Ready or not.

Just when he thought that all hope was gone, Nikki's legs started to quiver. Then they started to tremble. And at last, he was dealing with a full-blown earthquake.

But it wasn't clear who won because both exploded seemingly at the same time, Nikki with her sugar walls collapsing and Hylan with his dick jerking and jumping as it laced her neck with white pearls.

Breathing hard, he tilted over to the side and then rolled over onto his back.

Nikki reached over for her towel and cleaned herself up.

"Oh, baby girl. You could kill a man."

She laughed and then pumped up her fists. "Winner!"

"Winner?" He leaned up on his elbows. "What the hell are you talking about?"

"I made you come first," she declared.

"Did not!"

"Did so," she insisted. "You were all trembling and shaking like this." She jerked and writhed like someone having an epileptic episode.

"Ha-ha. Very funny—but that looked more like what you were doing," he countered, laughing. He sat up and repositioned himself so that he faced her. "But that's okay. I love it."

She hiked up her brows. "Really?"

"Really." He kissed her and ran his finger along the

dewy crease between her legs. "I hope that you don't think I'm finished with you."

"Funny." Nikki sat up. "I was just thinking the same thing about you."

"I think I've created a monster." Hylan pulled her close and rolled onto his back so that she could take the top position.

"Are you bragging or complaining?" she asked.

"Bragging. Definitely."

Straddling him, knees down, she gasped as she slid him all the way home. Hylan quickly filled his hands with her full, melon-shaped breasts just as she started bouncing. "Yes…oh!" He felt good. Damn good. Tears gathered and then streaked down her face. He filled her so completely that she would've sworn that his cock was bumping up against her heart.

Nikki closed her eyes and allowed his dick to become the center of her universe.

The strength.

The thickness.

The smoothness.

There was no doubt in her mind that her ass was sprung. Hard. Hylan could've asked her to rob a bank across the street from a police station at that moment and she would have done it without hesitation. He could have asked her to disown her family, donate a kidney or even leap off the Brooklyn Bridge, she would have done it all, as long as he promised to keep making love to her just like this, with a smile on her face.

Caught up and riding high from her body's sweetness, Hylan wondered for the first time in his life if there really was such a thing as voodoo, spells or hexes because something was happening to him that he simply couldn't explain. Something was taking a hold of his body, mind and spirit. Wasn't this the point where he was supposed to run like hell toward the exit door of this relationship? Wasn't he supposed to suddenly become too busy, thank her for a good time, and promise to call her soon?

As sure as he was breathing, he knew that he wasn't going to do any of that. He couldn't.

He sat up, grabbed her by the waist and flipped her over so he could beat it up doggy-style. Hands down, he knew that it was her favorite position. He could tell by the way she would buck and moan out his name. He smacked her on her perfectly round ass a few good times and got off on how it would jiggle around. But the more her sugar walls melted and dripped around his cock, the closer he was to climaxing.

"Tell me when you're about to come," he said. Sweat dotted along his hairline.

Smack! Smack! Smack!

"I don't wanna come unless you're coming," he panted.

Smack! Smack! Smack!

Nikki struggled to keep air in her lungs as she shot back, "You come first." She squeezed her vaginal muscles.

Smack! Smack! Smack!

Squeeze. Squeeze. Squeeze.

"Oh, you think you're slick." He reached around the

curve of her hip, rotated his fingers against her exposed clit while he continued to hit it from the back.

Nikki gasped. "Ch-cheater." Squeeze.

Smack!

Squeeze.

Smack!

But Nikki caught him slippin' because the next thing he knew his orgasm was seemingly rushing up from the tips of his toes at the speed of a locomotive. "Oh! Oh! Oh!"

"What's the matter, honey," Nikki asked, throwing her hip back with an extra oomph! "Cat got your tongue?" Squeeze. Squeeze.

As a matter of fact, it did. Hylan could no longer talk and could just barely breathe. When the moment was finally on him, he gave her ass one final smack and then jerked out of her creamy walls with a roar.

As Hylan's warm white pearls were tossed across her back, Nikki reached between her legs and found her bliss with just a couple more strokes. They collapsed, laughing and then Hylan had to give up the ghost and declare her the winner.

They lounged for a few minutes and then launched into an impromptu race back out in the rock pond under the waterfall. They played like Adam and Eve before they were cast out of paradise. There were no jobs, stress or worries about what tomorrow would bring. It was just them, living and loving in the moment.

Chapter 14

A two-week vacation was turning into a three-month sabbatical as June blazed into July and then drifted lazily into August. Hylan kept telling himself that it was time to go home, but every morning he woke up with Nikki curled up next to him, all thoughts of leaving vanished. Sometimes he struggled to understand the hold the eccentric woman had on him and other times he just gave up and decided to just roll with it. After all, he was a man who loved to live in the moment. And at this moment, he loved waking up with her by his side.

Every morning he was the first to wake up. It was his favorite time of day, when the early-dawn sunlight cut through the tall windows like shards of glass, bathing Nikki's beautiful skin with golden rays. She looked positively angelic, lying in a bed of Egyptian cotton sheets. He loved the way her dark hair spread like a halo over several pillows, just as he loved the fact that she clung to him during the night instead of the top sheet.

This morning, just like all the rest, one glance at her Coke-bottle curves increased the length of his erection. But he wouldn't wake her. Not yet anyway. Right now, he just wanted to drink his fill of her. He stared at her bare face, mesmerized by its sun-kissed perfection. Her eyelashes were incredibly long and had a natural curl. Her nose was a bit short, straight at the base and small at the tip. Her lips were one of her best features—full, lush and always soft, begging to be kissed.

Then there was her neck—incredibly long and sensuous. It could bring out the vampire in any man. Without thinking, he reached out and lightly brushed his finger across her collarbone. Almost immediately, he noticed the quick acceleration of her heartbeat from the pulse in her neck.

I wouldn't mind doing this for the rest of my life.

Hylan's fingers stopped midstroke. Where had that thought come from? He tried to shrug it off. But it wasn't working, maybe because it was the truth. "What have you done to me?"

At the sound of his voice, Nikki's eyes fluttered open. She smiled when their gazes locked. "How come every time I wake up you're staring at me?"

"Because you're beautiful," he said and then pressed a kiss against her lips.

She giggled and turned her head away. "Stop. You know I have morning breath." She turned away and started to climb out of bed.

Hylan wasn't having it. He whipped an arm around her waist and dragged her back. "You have no such thing." He pinned her beneath him.

Nikki pushed at his chest in a futile attempt to get away. "Liar."

"Look who's calling the kettle black." He kneed her legs open.

"Why, Mr. Dawson, you sure are horny in the mornings."

"Last time I checked, *Mrs. Dawson,* so were you." He entered her with one swift thrust of his hips.

Nikki arched her head back against the pillows. What she was feeling went beyond pleasure as her body responded with its usual quakes and tremors.

Hylan feasted on her neck while her breasts jiggled against his chest. He was addicted. There was no point in denying it anymore. Never in his adult life had he ever spent this much time with one woman—nor had he wanted to. Somewhere along the way while they were playing house, it all started to feel real to him. He wanted this woman more than he wanted water to drink, food to eat or even air to breathe.

Nothing about the way they met or had fallen in love made sense. *Wait. Did I just say* love?

Hylan's steady, deep strokes slowed as he lifted his head and stared down at her.

Nikki noticed the sudden change in their lovemaking and lowered her head so she could return his curious stare. "Is something wrong, baby?" she panted.

His confusion was etched into the small lines in his face.

"Baby?" she asked again.

I love her, he repeated to himself. He couldn't believe it. A smile blossomed across his face and his hips returned to their regularly scheduled program. "Nothing's wrong, baby. Everything is just perfect."

She smiled before her eyes fluttered closed again so she could luxuriate in the wondrous feelings he was arousing in her. More than once, he brought her to the brink of ecstasy only to change the rhythm and prolong the ecstasy. He finally allowed the slow building of her first orgasm. She thrashed mindlessly and clawed at his back.

Hylan grabbed her legs, jacked them up over his shoulders and started pounding away. He could feel her body's juices drip down the lower part of his groin and he could feel her vaginal muscles pulse to his rhythm.

"Hylan," she recited while she struggled to catch her breath. And then, "I'm coming." She screamed his name one last time before her body exploded and she went limp in his arms. Seconds later, she heard Hylan's mighty roar and felt him collapse behind her.

He gathered her close and returned to raining kisses along the nape of her neck.

"I love you," he panted softly.

Nikki's eyes fluttered open as a smile caressed her lips. "I love you, too," she said, and meant it.

Later that afternoon, Hylan and Nikki flittered around the kitchen, trying to figure out what to make for lunch. What started out as a friendly debate over whether to grill or just throw together a salad, ended in a food fight. It seemed like it was going to be the one contest that Nikki could win. She managed to dodge ingredients like sliced cucumbers, lettuce and cherry tomatoes while Hylan was nailed with a couple of globs of raw hamburger meat.

"Oh, you think you're funny," Hylan said and grabbed fistfuls of iceberg lettuce, launching them at her.

"You're cheating," she shouted. Nikki ran to the refrigerator and grabbed the first thing she could lay her hands on—eggs.

"Whoa, whoa," he said, holding up his hands. "What do you think you're going to do with those?"

"What do you think?" Nikki laughed and then launched the first egg torpedo at him.

He ducked and heard the splat against the cabinet behind him. "Ah. It's going to be like that, huh? Well then I got something for you," he said, and then quickly launched two ground beef cannonballs at her.

Squealing, she took off running. One hit the refrigerator with a *thunk!* The second one nailed her right shoulder.

"Yeah, baby!" He pumped his fist in victory.

But Nikki didn't waste any time launching her counterattack. While Hylan was doing a premature victory dance, she pumped four eggs in quick recession, each one found its mark on his head, face and chest.

He roared as his hands fell down to block his face, it was already too late. Egg yolk dripped down in front of his face in a slimy curtain. "I'm going to get you!" And he took off after her. Seeing his massive form race toward her, Nikki screamed, dropped the carton of eggs and ran like hell.

Ding-dong!

Saved by the bell. "Time out. Time out. There's somebody at the door." She turned, holding her hands up in a tee formation, signaling time out but still found herself in the midst of an all-out assault. Hylan had the presence of mind to tuck and roll so that when they tumbled to the floor, he absorbed most of the impact.

Nikki shrieked with laughter when Hylan proceeded to try and tickle her to death.

Ding-dong!

"Th-the door," she panted. "We've got to get to the door."

"Screw the door. Do you give up?" It was clear that he wanted to win.

"N-no!" She laughed and giggled and tried wiggling away.

"What?" He redoubled his efforts, tickling her sides, her lower belly and even under her arms.

She swatted at his hands. "No fair."

"All is fair in love and war, sweetheart. Now let me hear you say it."

"N-no!"

"We can stay like this all night. Do you give up?"

Nikki laughed so hard, she started to ache. Tears rolled in fat droplets down the side of her face. She wasn't going to be able to hold out much longer.

Ding-dong!

"All right. All right. I give up," she shouted.

Again Hylan's fists pumped in the air. "Victory! Yess!"

Still laughing, Nikki pulled herself up and then punched him playfully in his chest. "You're a cheater is what you are."

Ding-dong!

"And I told you that there was someone at the door," she pouted as she rose to her feet.

"Aw. You're not going to start crying now, too, are you?" He poked out his bottom lip.

Nikki marched over to the front door. "I'm coming. I'm coming." She snatched open the door, but the smile on her face evaporated. "Mom! Dad!"

Chapter 15

"Don't forget me," Barbara piped up, waving from behind their parents.

Nikki just stared. "What are you guys doing here?"

"What do you think we're doing here?" Her mother frowned. "What do you mean? You ran off and got married and we haven't seen you for almost two years."

Her father nodded. "Since you refuse to bring this young man home to meet us, we figured that we'd come here. Now are you going to invite us in or leave us standing outside, looking silly?"

Nikki's thoughts were tripping over themselves as she continued to stand and stare like the village idiot.

"Who's at the door, honey?" Hylan asked, walking

into view while still wiping food from his head and face. "Oh, hello." He smiled. "Can we help you?"

"Oh, my. He is handsome," Mrs. Jamison said, pushing her daughter out the way and storming into the house so she could take a good look at her son-in-law. "You're so tall," she commented, making a circle around him.

"Um…thanks." He eyed the woman who was giving him a 360-degree inspection. Then he caught the resemblance. His questioning gaze then swung to the still shell-shocked Nikki.

"Your parents?" he asked.

"What—you didn't think she had any?" her father snapped. His dark eyes raked over Hylan and didn't appear to like what he saw.

Ella clapped her hands once and then threw them around Hylan and gave him a bear hug. "It's so nice to finally meet you."

Hylan, not sure what to do, awkwardly lowered the towel from his face and hugged the woman back. "I-it's nice to finally meet you, too."

"Uh-huh." Wilbur Jamison rocked back on his heels. "Seems to me that the man didn't even know who we were." His disappointed face shifted to his older daughter. "Which is understandable since he did not grant us the common courtesy of introducing himself and asking me for my daughter's hand."

Hylan groaned. *Oh this about to be a nightmare.*

"So are you going to give us a proper introduction or not?" Wilbur asked Nikki.

"O-of course." Nikki fluttered a weak smile. "Mom,

Dad, this is my—" she cleared her throat "—my husband, Hylan. Hylan, these are my parents, Ella and Wilbur Jamison."

Hylan tilted his head. "How do you do?"

Barbara reached over and tapped her older sister on the shoulder. "Don't forget about me."

"Oh um, and this is my baby sister, Barbara," she added.

"Ah. You're nearly as beautiful as my wife," he teased.

Barbara fluttered her lashes demurely. "Good going, sis," she whispered conspiratorially.

Nikki avoided her sister's twinkling gaze and said, "So, um, come on in," she finally said, pulling the door all the way back so everyone could enter. "Hylan, maybe you could help them with their bags."

"Good idea." He pried himself out Ella's arms and rushed out the door to the cab. All the while, his mind was racing. What the hell were they going to do now?

Barbara gushed at her older sister as she gave her a soft jab of her elbow. "His pictures don't do him justice," she whispered.

Guilt and shame continued to pile onto Nikki's shoulders. The only reason she'd told her parents that she'd gotten married was because Barbara had called the house one day and actually spoke to Mahina. Mahina had referred to her as Mrs. Dawson and before she had a chance to talk to Barbara, she had already called and told her folks. So the lie just continued to grow.

"Why didn't you guys tell me that you were coming?"

she asked, still trying to stifle the panic that was rising in her chest.

"Because you would have told us not to come," her mother reasoned.

Damn right.

"This is a gorgeous place," he mother continued, looking around. "Not to mention that it's smack dab in the middle of paradise, too." She glanced at her husband. "Your father thought that you were shut away in some shack."

Wilbur harrumphed and stiffened his back. "Well, something had to be up. The child was behaving strangely. Stranger than normal, that is."

Nikki's chin came up at the backhanded barb. "As you can see, I'm fine. So if you came all this way to—"

"Now, now," her mother stepped in. "Everybody just take a breath. Nobody came here to do anything other than welcome that nice young man into the family." She smiled and pushed back Nikki's hair from her face. "Surely, you know that we've missed you."

Nikki smiled, but it was heavy—just like the guilt that continued to pile on.

Hylan returned to the house with his arms loaded down with bags. "I guess I'll just take these up to the guest room," he said.

"I'll help," Nikki offered. She needed a few minutes to apologize for this latest development.

"We'll all come," Nikki's mom announced. "Since we'll need to know where we'll be sleeping for the next two weeks."

"Two weeks," Hylan and Nikki thundered.

"Is that a problem?" Wilbur asked, his brows hiking in suspicion.

Nikki and Hylan's gaze jerked toward one another.

"Um, no. Two weeks is fine," Nikki lied. "We're thrilled to have you."

"Great." Ella clapped her hands together gleefully. "See, Wilbur. I told you that everything was going work out just fine. This is going to be the best vacation. Who knows, we probably will never want to leave."

Hylan and Nikki looked as if they'd both been handed a death sentence.

"Well, lead the way, Mr. Dawson," Wilbur said, grabbing the bags that he'd carried from the cab.

"Okay," Hylan said, then, under his breath added, "This should be fun." He turned and led his new in-laws up the main staircase.

Barbara looped her arms possessively through Nikki's and leaned in close to whisper, "I can see why you'd want to keep him hidden away. He's fine."

Nikki didn't respond. There was no way she was going to be able to keep a fake marriage together under her parent's watchful eyes—especially her father. He was like a human detective. Nothing ever got past him.

Sensing that her older sister was worried, Barbara added, "Don't worry about Dad. You know that his bark is worse than his bite. He's just hurt that he wasn't invited to your wedding. To be honest, so was I," she whispered as they climbed the stairs.

"What?"

"C'mon. What were you thinking? I know that you were really down and out after your play…um, didn't do so well."

"You mean when it bombed," Nikki corrected.

"Yeah. When that happened, I know that you were at a low point in your life, but I never once thought you would just pack up and leave the way you did. In some ways I was angry, but in other ways I so admired you for it."

Nikki couldn't believe what she was hearing. "You admired me?"

"Are you kidding? I've always admired you. You're never afraid of taking risks. They don't always work out, but hey, it's better than always doing the safe thing—the sensible thing." Barbara huffed out tired breath. "When you left, you weren't ashamed of us or something?"

"What? No. Of course not."

Barbara fell silent for a moment. "You know, growing up I always imagined that we would be each other's maid of honor. Sort of a sister thing. You know."

Tears burned Nikki's eyes. "Look, Barbara. I—"

"But you know what?" her sister said. "All that matters is that you're happy. It's been a long time since I've seen a smile like the one you had when you opened the door. You were positively glowing. You're not pregnant, are you?"

Nikki nearly tripped over her own feet. "What?"

"Whoa. Be careful," Barbara said, catching her by the arm.

"Are you okay, hon?" Hylan asked even though he was several feet down the hall from her.

"Oh she's fine. I caught her," Barbara said cheerily and then added for her sister's ears only, "He's definitely a keeper."

Nikki lowered her voice. "What makes you ask if I'm pregnant?"

Barbara clasped her hands together. "Did I guess right?"

"No," Nikki said, feeling her face drain of blood. But as she was doing the calculations in her head, she didn't know whether she was trying to convince her sister or herself.

"Well, if I lived in the middle of paradise with a husband that looked like that, I'd be trying to pump out a house full of babies."

Hylan's new father-in-law didn't like him. That much was clear.

It didn't matter how nice he was, how many jokes he tried to crack or how he took each of Wilbur's backhanded remarks with a smile, Wilbur Jamison had made up his mind. Things only got worse when Hylan's family dropped by once again. It seemed word had gotten out about the Jamisons's visit and everyone figured that they would drop by and make their own introductions. Before Nikki and Hylan knew it, they were hosting a full-fledged house party.

Nikki, however was on pins and needles because there was no way to control or stop her mountain of lies from slipping into her parents' ear. And she didn't have that long to wait.

"Let me get this straight," Wilbur said suddenly.

"You mean to tell me that Nicole has been living here on the island by herself for the first eighteen months of your marriage?" His gaze stabbed Hylan just as he was handing Rafiq and a couple of cousins bottles of beer. "Where the hell were you all that time?"

"I, um—" he looked to Nikki "—I was working in Atlanta."

Wilbur glared. "Now I may be getting on in years, but back when I was still working a nine-to-five, I still came home to my wife and family every evening."

"Preach on it," Aunt Addie chimed in.

A few more heads bobbed in agreement.

"So you just married her and then stashed her away here on the island?" Wilbur asked.

"Daddy," Nikki said, smiling. "It was nothing like that."

"Hush, baby," her father said. "I'm talking to your husband, man-to-man."

"Wilbur," Ella cooed. "Drop it. You're causing a scene."

"What? I'm just trying to get to the bottom of some things. Our daughter disappears for two years. I think we have a right to know what's been going on with her. Lord knows we're not going to get a straight answer from her. Every time we called here, she just said that he was out—not gone."

"Wilbur," Ella hissed.

"At first I thought the rushed marriage meant that she'd gotten knocked up or something but that wasn't the case."

The party had fallen silent as everyone watched Nikki's father grow more heated by the second.

"For the last time, Wilbur, you are embarrassing everyone."

"Oh okay. So I'm not supposed to say what everyone else is thinking? C'mon. We both know that Nikki doesn't exactly make the best decisions. That includes everything from career choices to…to men." He turned his attention back to his daughter. "Now I love you, but this whole thing has me mad as hell and I want some damn answers."

Nikki dropped her head, but not before Hylan witnessed tears shining in her eyes. Hylan walked over to his wife and draped an arm around her drooping shoulders. "Mr. Jamison, I truly understand your concern and you're entitled to your opinions. I know that you love your daughter, but I'm now going to ask, respectfully, for you to shut the hell up."

Everyone gasped.

"What?" Wilbur thundered. His fists balled against his hips and his eyes turned a murderous hue.

"I think you heard me." Hylan thrust up his chin and chest and refused to back down.

Wilbur took a step forward.

Ella grabbed him by the waist. "Wilbur, calm down."

Hylan took a step forward.

Nikki grabbed him by the waist. "Don't, Hylan. Please."

"Look, Mr. Jamison. Whether you want to believe it or not, I love your daughter. And I'm not about to stand here and let you berate her like you usually do. Not here. Not in our home."

Wilbur's chin came up. "Is that what she said? That I berate her?"

"You've been doing it since you walked through that door and I have had enough."

"I only want what's best for my daughters," Wilbur gritted out through his clenched teeth. "And I'm not sure that you fit that bill just yet."

"And I—"

"Hylan, let's just tell—"

"No, baby. Let me finish," Hylan insisted. His arm remained locked around her shoulder. "Sure. Nikki has made some mistakes in her life. We all have. But I happen to think that it takes guts to follow your passion—and like it or not, writing is her passion. And frankly, I'm proud that she's sticking with it."

"Is that what's she's been doing out here—writing?" His sharp eyes swung toward Nikki. "I thought you would've gotten that out of your system after that last disaster that wiped out our bank account."

Ella groaned in disbelief. "Wilbur." She sniffed and shook her head.

"Do you need me to write you a check?" Hylan asked, coldly.

"What?"

Hylan reached into his back pocket and withdrew his checkbook. "Should I toss in her college expenses, too?" He glanced over at Mahina. "Get me a pen."

Nikki's head jerked up. "Hylan, don't—"

"It's all right, baby. I want to."

"Baby, I can't let you—"

"I don't want your damn money," Wilbur snapped. "It's not about the money. It's never been about the money."

"Really? Have you ever told her that?" Hylan challenged.

Wilbur's mouth flapped wordlessly. Then there was a dawning light in his eyes as he looked back at his daughter. "I-I didn't think I needed to."

"Yeah, you did." Hylan said, and then pressed a kiss on top of Nikki's head.

Ella and Barbara beamed at Hylan.

"You really do love her, don't you?" Ella asked as tears gathered in her eyes.

He looked down at the woman in his arms. His heart tugged as he confessed, "I do."

"Then that's a good thing," Wilbur said. "Or I would've had to punch your lights out for talking to me like that."

Hylan shifted his gaze back and saw the man smile for the first time.

"As it turns out, you might have made a good point." Wilbur tried to take another step, but then had to look down and said, "You can release me now, Ella. I'm not going to hurt the young man."

"I was more worried that he was going to hurt you," she mumbled, releasing him.

A few people snickered.

Nikki also released Hylan so he could cross the room and enfold her father in a bear hug. The room exploded into applause.

Nikki smiled, but she needed to sit down. As heartwarming as this scene was, she knew that she was just moments away from cracking under the weight of her lies. However, just the thought of blurting the truth made her feel equally sick. Everyone would hate her—no, loathe her.

"You know, she really is a good writer," Hylan boasted to the group surrounding him and her father.

"Isn't this wonderful?" Barbara asked, settling down next to Nikki on the sofa. "Dad and Hylan getting along? I can't believe it. I've been engaged to Clifford for over two years and I've yet to see those two hug."

Nikki frowned. "Why haven't you married your little neurosurgeon?"

"Why?" Barbara echoed and then shifted un-comfortably under her sister's gaze.

"Yeah, why?"

Barbara rolled her eyes across the room. "Because Clifford is no Hylan Dawson."

"Excuse me?"

"Don't get me wrong." Barbara hastily added. "I'm not trying to…you know go after your man or anything like that. It's just that. Well, look at him. He's tall and muscular—not to mention charming. I bet life with him has got to be exciting, huh?"

Nikki shrugged and thought about the past three months that she and Hylan had been playing house and had to admit that there hadn't been a dull moment. She helped him get reconnected with family and introduced him to neighbors that he didn't know he had. He helped rebuild her confidence and inspired her to finally complete a new play. And they had fun, laughing and playing—both in and out of the bedroom.

"It has been exciting," she admitted.

"See. I don't get that with Clifford." Barbara suddenly looked sad. "And he probably doesn't get it from me either."

"Are you all right?" Nikki swung an arm around her baby sister.

Barbara shook her head before bursting out with, "We're boring!" She sniffed. "I mean—our lives are just so structured. Up by five and in bed by nine thirty. Sure, we make good money and live in a nice house but we never do anything. And the sex," she said, grabbing Nikki's hand. "It's awful."

Sympathetic, Nikki knew exactly what her sister was going through. After all, she'd been there herself. "Oh, Barbara. I had no idea."

Her sister swiped at her tears. "You have no idea how much I envy you."

"Envy me?" Nikki couldn't believe what she was hearing.

"You've never been afraid to take risks," Barbara said. "When you set your mind on doing something, you just do it. By hook or by crook. If you didn't like something, you'd just change up and pursue something else. I wish I was as brave as you are."

Nikki nearly laughed aloud. "Believe me. I'm not all that brave."

"Please. One day you decide to leave New York and the next day you're gone. That's brave. And look what happened? You now live in a Caribbean paradise with a man that could be a centerfold in *Playgirl*."

Nikki dropped her head. "Look, Barbara. About that. I think that there's something you should know."

"What? You're a Kappa Psi Kappa?" Wilbur roared above the crowd. "Nikki, how come you didn't tell me you married a Kappa man?"

Nikki's jerked up. "Um…I guess it sort of slipped my mind."

"I'm a Kappa Psi Kappa, too," Wilbur announced and then immediately launched into some old fraternity moves from his old stepping days.

Nikki and Barbara were just seconds away from dying in embarrassment when Hylan busted out a few of his own moves.

"Oh my God," Nikki and Barbara said, laughing along with the crowd.

The men gave each other dabs and another bear hug. "Well all right!" Wilbur boasted. "Another Kappa man in the family."

"I think Daddy is going to steal your husband," Barbara whispered.

I wish he was mine to steal.

"And here I was giving you a hard time."

Ding-dong!

"I'll get it," Momma Mahina said, threading through the crowd, grinning.

Nikki couldn't imagine who it could be. It seemed that everyone in the quarter was already there.

Ding-dong!

"I'm coming. I'm coming," Mahina said, rushing.

But when she snatched back the door, her joyous mood disappeared when she recognized the woman on the other side of the door.

"Hi, Mahina. How are you?" the woman said, throwing her arms around the stout maid. "I can't believe that you're still working here."

Mahina just blinked and stared.

"Is Hylan home?"

"He's…in the living room."

"Great." She sashayed off before Mahina thought to stop her.

"Hylan," the woman sing-songed as she rounded the corner. "Guess who—" She froze when she noticed the packed house. "Oh, you're throwing a party?"

Nikki's gaze also zeroed in on the stunningly beautiful woman dressed in a bikini and sarong. Jealousy delivered a high karate chop right in the center of her gut. She knew without being told exactly who this woman was to Hylan.

Once again, everything stopped as Hylan slowly turned toward what was about to turn into a nightmare. "Shonda."

Chapter 16

"Hylan, honey?" Shonda said. "Why is everybody looking at me?"

Hylan tried to stomp down his panic as he carefully eased away from Mr. Jamison. "Um, excuse me." However, he hadn't made more than a few steps when Wilbur barked out to him.

"Are you going to introduce us to your friend?"

Nikki jumped up, fully intending to smooth things over with an "Everything is all right, she's a friend of the family" lie, but her emotions choked off her words and all that she could manage was a mix between a sob and a whimper. In her defense, it wasn't every day a woman had to defend her husband's lover—or rather defend her fake husband's lover. Either way, this Shonda chick was someone he'd gotten lost in at some other time.

Hylan was stumped by the question. "Shonda is…a friend." He cut a look over to Nikki and watched as raw pain etched into her beautiful face. "An old friend," he added, thinking the added adjective would help but it only seemed to shove his foot farther down his throat.

Shonda, on the other hand, looked pissed. "Oh, I'm just a friend now?" she asked, rocking her neck and jamming her hands onto her hips.

Hylan gritted his teeth. "Can we please take this outside?"

Finding her stubborn streak, Shonda folded her arms and made it clear that she was comfortable just where she was standing. "I just came in from outside."

The first wave of nausea caught Nikki off guard. She'd just barely slapped a hand across her mouth to stop herself from tossing up all the green figs and salt fish she'd been nibbling on throughout the party.

"Are you all right?" Barbara asked, jumping to her feet and wrapping an arm around her sister's waist.

Nikki closed her eyes and waited for her stomach to settle down a bit.

Momma Mahina stepped in. "Now where did all the music go? Rafiq?"

Her nephew frowned. Clearly he didn't want to turn the music back on because that would mean he and his cousins could potentially miss out on some key elements of this unfolding drama.

"Rafiq!" Momma Mahina snapped.

"Yes, ma'am," He reached over and turned the music up.

But no one tore their eyes away from Shonda and Hylan.

"Don't start anything, I can explain everything later," Hylan hissed, reaching for her arm.

Shonda jerked back as if she could already see the writing on the wall. "Filming wrapped up in L.A. I heard that you were still out here at your vacation home so I figured I'd cash in on that invitation."

"This isn't a good time," he said.

"Nonsense, son," Wilbur smacked him *hard* on the back. "It's a party. The more the merrier." His hard gaze shifted to Shonda.

Nikki saw what was about to happen but was unable to stop it.

"I'm Wilbur Jamison," her father said extending a hand. "I'm Hylan's father-in-law?"

"FATHER-IN-LAW?" Shonda's neck swiveled like a cobra. "YOU'RE MARRIED?"

And the music went back off.

"Shonda—"

"When the fuck did you get married?"

"Shonda—"

"Almost two years ago," Wilbur supplied, folding his arms. "Isn't that right, son?"

All cheeriness and brotherhood unity had evaporated from the man's black gaze and in its place raged an anger so intense that Hylan suspected that he was just seconds away from getting his ass whipped. "Now, Wilbur, I can explain—"

"TWO YEARS!" Shonda screeched.

Nikki was dizzy.

"WHERE THE HELL YOU GET OFF BEING MARRIED FOR TWO YEARS?"

"It's Mister Jamison. And I would really love to hear your explanation." He looked up at the surrounding crowd and barked. "EVERYBODY OUT!"

It was a command that made it clear there was no room for argument. There were a few grumblings and a large number of disappointed faces cast at Hylan, while Nikki got her fair share of sympathetic glances and hugs.

"You hang in there," a few of the women whispered. But there were also comments like, "I told you that something was up with him being gone so long," whispered by others.

On the way out, Rafiq stopped by Hylan and shook his head. "I'm so disappointed, man."

Hylan just took a deep breath and hung his head.

"I CAN'T BELIEVE THIS, YOU SORRY SON OF A BITCH!"

"Wait!" Nikki said, finally rushing over to the fray. "I can—"

"Nikki, let me handle this," her father barked.

"YOU WERE MARRIED ALL THIS TIME WE WERE TOGETHER?"

"Not exactly," Hylan tried to explain.

"Not exactly?" Wilbur thundered. "Either you're married or you're not."

"Exactly."

Hylan finally glanced over to Nikki for some help.

"Daddy, there's something that I need to tell you. Hylan and I—"

"Will be getting a divorce," her father finished for her.

"No need for a divorce," Shonda sneered. "Your daughter can have his ass." She pivoted with the flair of a fierce supermodel rocking a catwalk and finally stormed out of the house.

This can't be happening, Hylan thought to himself. Everything was spiraling at a crazy pace. He turned toward Mr. Jamison, ready to finally come clean when Wilbur delivered a punch to his jaw that damn near lifted him off the ground.

"Daddy!" Nikki shrieked and raced over to Hylan, who'd hit the wall behind him and was sinking down to the floor.

Momma Mahina and Aunt Addie rushed back through the door. "Oh, Hylan!"

Wilbur shook out the pain in his hand and went over and pulled his daughter away from Hylan. "Trust me, sweetheart. You'll thank me later."

"Daddy, you didn't have to hurt him!" Nikki struggled and squirmed, trying to get out of his embrace.

Mahina pried open Hylan's eyes. "Are you all right?"

Hylan groaned, mainly because it felt like his jaw was broken.

"Rafiq!" Mahina shouted. "Someone get Rafiq."

"Yeah. Somebody come and get this jerk out of here," Wilbur thundered. "Nobody treats my daughter this way."

That woke Hylan up. "W-what? B-but this is my house."

Wilbur took a threatening step forward.

"Daddy!" Nikki clutched at her father just as the room started spinning around her.

Hylan forgot about the pain in his jaw as he watched Nikki swoon forward. "Nikki!"

Being the closest to her, Wilbur spun around and caught his daughter before she hit the floor. "Nicole, darling. Are you all right?" He gave her a small pat on the face. She stirred a bit but not much.

Hylan wobbled to his feet and tried to reach her.

"No!" Wilbur barked. "You get out."

"Mr. Jamison, there's something you should know."

"NOW!"

Ella and Barbara rushed around Nikki and Wilbur.

Helpless, Hylan's hands fell to his sides. No way was this man going to believe anything he was going to say right now. But he stood there until he saw Nikki's eyes flutter open. She was disoriented for a second, but then her eyes immediately searched for him in the room. The combination of pain and tears were enough to do him in.

"All right. I'll go."

Chapter 17

On a typical Atlanta Saturday morning, Taariq strolled through the doors of Herman's Barbershop. Lately, it was the only place that he and the Kappa brothers got in any male bonding time. With Derrick and Charlie wrapped in harmonious marital bliss and Hylan still M.I.A. in Saint Lucia, Taariq was left hanging with Stanley—which was not a good look.

"Yo, Taariq!" the entire crowd in the shop shouted.

"Mornin'," he gave everyone a short salute.

"You're late," Herman Keillor, the shop's owner, said, peeking over a pair of wire-rimmed glasses.

Taariq glanced at his watch and saw that he was indeed five minutes late. "Sorry about that, old man. I'll do better next time." He winked.

"Make sure that you do. You know I don't like any of that CP Time nonsense."

The guys gathered around the mounted twenty-seven-inch television chuckled at the backhanded complaint and then returned their attention to *SportsCenter*.

Herman, a tall, robust gentleman, had owned the shop for over forty years. The old red brick building was a staple in the community. Most men drifted through to hear Herman's stories, tough love advice and get sharp haircuts.

Taariq wasn't originally from ATL, but learned about the place through his Kappa brother, Derrick. The first one in their clique to turn in his playa card for a woman who was technically engaged to marry a prominent politician and fellow Kappa Psi Kappa brother, Randall Jarrett. After rescuing him from a kidnapping situation, Derrick arrived in time to save his future wife from making the biggest mistake of her life.

Of course there was that funny incident with Derrick, Randall and Reverend Williams falling headfirst into a Lady Justice water fountain and duking it out in the front of Washington's political elite. Good times.

"Come on over," Herman directed. "I got your seat all warmed and ready."

Taariq strolled over and plopped into the leather chair.

The bell above the door continued to jiggle as men from the neighborhood filtered in and out, some to get their hair cut and some just to watch the television. Saturday had always been Herman's busiest day of the week. Six barbers ranging from old school to new school donned burgundy barber jackets with Herman's name scrawled across the back.

"So what's been happening, Taariq?" Herman asked, smiling and draping a black smock around his neck.

"Just been chillin', I guess."

"Well that's good. Don't want to overdo it."

J.T., the local street hustler, pimped walked his way into the door and made a beeline over to Taariq. "T, my main man. You know I got you today, baby."

"Oh, really? What you got?"

"Lookee here. I know you're a ladies man, so I got you the latest Beyonce and Alicia Keys." He reached into his magic jacket and produced two CDs. "Bam! What you think about those?"

Taariq shook his head. "Nah, these two ladies are a bit too young for me."

"Too young? Man, you trippin'." J.T. stuffed the CDs back into his pocket.

"Nah." He glanced around. "Ayo, where's Bobby?"

"Lord knows," Herman said, shaking his head. "His ass is late, too."

"Hey didn't school just start? Maybe you should cut the college kid a break."

"I'm cutting him a check for that damn tuition. The least he could do is show up for work on time."

Sensing he'd wandered into sensitive territory with Herman's grandson, Taariq tossed up his hands. "Sorry 'bout that. I didn't mean no harm. I was just trying to stick up for a fellow Kappa man. You understand."

"Uh-huh." Herman clicked on his clippers.

The shop's bell jiggled again, but this time it was

Derrick and Charlie strolling through like regular rock stars. They were greeted with a round of perfunctory, "Yo, whassup?"

"Hey, what's happening, captain?" Taariq asked, grinning.

"You got it," Charlie said.

His boys made it over to his chair and exchanged a couple of fist bumps.

J.T. popped his head back up. "What about some DVDs?"

"Will you get out of here with that," Charlie said, laughing. "You know we never buy none of that bootleg crap. Why do you keep asking?"

"Close mouth don't get fed," J.T. reasoned.

Derrick shrugged. "The man makes sense."

The door jiggled again and a smiling Stanley strolled inside. None of the regulars called the lanky redhead by his first name. Instead, they affectionately called the man "Breadstick" and sometimes "Whitey"—mainly because he was still the only white man to get his hair cut at Herman's.

"Yo, everybody, whassup?" Stanley said in his best Vanilla Ice impersonation. Everyone was used to the white man who thought he was black and just hollered back at him.

"Looks like we're all here," Taariq said.

Derrick frowned. "You mean Hylan is still not back yet?"

The Kappas shook their heads.

"Hell, has he even bothered to check in?" he asked. "It's not like him to be gone this long."

"He left me a message a while back," Taariq remembered and pulled out his cell phone. "I haven't had a chance to call him back."

"Get that man on the phone," Charlie said. "At least so that we know his ass is still breathing."

Taariq held up a hand. "Herman, could you hold on a second?"

Herman cut off his clippers. "Sure. I live to wait on you guys," he joked.

Taariq found Hylan's home number in his cell's address book and hit the call button. A second later the line was ringing. Then a woman answered the phone. "Hello, is Hylan there?"

"No. I'm sorry he's not. This is his sister-in-law, Barbara. Can I take a message?"

Taariq pulled the phone away from his ear for a moment and stared at it.

"What's wrong?" The Kappa boys asked in unison.

"Um, yeah," Taariq said putting the phone back to his ear. "Just tell him that Taariq called."

"Oh, would you like to talk to his wife?"

"Uh, no. That, um, won't be necessary. I'll just get in touch with him later." He disconnected the call.

"What was that all about?" Stanley asked.

Taariq looked up. "Guys, how do y'all feel about making a trip to the Caribbean to meet Hylan's wife?"

Nikki was pregnant.

The nausea and the dizziness might have been her first clue, but the fourth pregnancy test really hammered the point home. *What am I going to do?* She must've asked herself that question about every other minute and so far, she had yet to come up with an answer.

"Are you happy?" Barbara asked, gently.

Nikki lifted her head from the toilet and stared at her sister with tear-brimmed eyes. "Ecstatic."

"You're being sarcastic," Barbara deduced with a roll of her eyes. "I'm serious."

Nikki pulled herself off the floor. "Barbara, to be honest, I don't know how I feel and I don't know what to do." Last night, she'd finally taken the plunge and confided in her sister about her fake marriage. Her baby sister took the news with her mouth sagging open and her eyes as wide as last night's full moon.

Nikki apologized profusely for lying to her, but explained how everything just snowballed out of control—especially when her husband showed up.

"But why did he go along with it?" Barbara finally asked.

"He said he liked me."

That was all it took for Barbara to adore her fake brother-in-law. "Does he like you or does he love you?"

Nikki's mind quickly recounted the number of times Hylan had said he loved her. Did he mean it casually or did he mean that he was in love with her?

"I mean, he even told Daddy that he loved you, right?" Barbara campaigned. "Surely that's a big deal, even for a supposed ladies' man. I would imagine that they would go out of their way not to say those words."

"Yeah, I guess," Nikki said, turned on the faucet and dosing her face with cold water.

"Well, how do you feel about him?"

Nikki went still with her face still cupped in her water-filled hands. There had been no question whatsoever how she felt about Hylan. She loved him. She was in love with him, probably had been since before he'd even shown up there.

"Never mind," Barbara said. "I believe I already know the answer."

"It's complicated," Nikki said, straightening and reaching for a face towel.

"I don't know. It sounds simple enough. You fell in love with your fake husband."

Nikki laughed and moved from the bathroom to the bed.

Barbara followed and folded her arms. "And now you're about to have his kid. Don't you think you should at least tell him?"

"What, so he will do the honorable thing? No thanks. I've already duped him into one fake marriage. I don't want to trap him into a real one."

Chapter 18

It had been two days and Hylan still couldn't believe that he'd been kicked out of his own house by a family that really wasn't related to him. And to make matters worse, everybody in Soufrière now treated him like he had the plague. Everywhere he went people glared and shook their heads as if to say how dare he cheat on their beloved angel.

But how could he defend himself? To call Nikki a fraud now would be a bit disingenuous, seeing how he'd gone along with it for the past three months. Three months. What the hell was he thinking?

I wasn't thinking. I was feeling.

"A lot that does me now," he said, arguing with himself. He at least needed to see her, but her watchdog of a father wouldn't let him get anywhere near her. And when he asked his own family members or longtime employee to pass his wife a note, he'd been turned down. It was like he was in some type of *Twilight Zone*, where up was down and down was up.

One thing was for sure, he needed to do something.

I could just cut my losses and head back home. Let her explain to her family why she couldn't file for a divorce. That idea wasn't even the least bit tempting. He didn't want to leave without her...even though that had been the game plan all along. But people changed their plans all the time, he reasoned. There was no reason why they couldn't either. After all, he loved her.

No. I'm in love with her.

He laughed at himself. This was the feeling that he's been trying to avoid all these years? This wonderful warmth that spread throughout his body whenever he thought about the woman he loves—or how about the ache to just touch her that he'd felt the past two mornings? The very idea of never being able to hold, touch, kiss or even make love to her was making him physically ill.

Nicole Dawson. Nikki Dawson. They actually had a nice ring to them. He laughed again. "I don't believe I'm thinking what I'm thinking," he said.

Lathan shuffled through the living room, strapping his tool belt onto his narrow frame even though he was still in his pajamas. It was a strange habit Hylan noticed he had for the past two days. Mahina's husband wore it just in case he had to fix something around the house.

"You had breakfast yet?" Lathan asked as he headed to the kitchen.

Hylan pulled the sheet back and sat up from the sofa he'd been borrowing since he'd been kicked out. "Nah. Not yet. I've just been lying here…thinking." He watched the old man shake his head and drag his feet so his house shoes scuffled across the floor.

"Shouldn't be much to think about," Lathan said. "I think that everybody knows what you need to do. You just need to hurry up and do it." He made it to the coffeemaker.

Did the man always talk in circles first thing in the morning?

Thirty seconds later, the fresh aroma of coffee wafted through the small house and put a smile on both men's faces. Since he'd already taken a shower the night before, Hylan hopped up and in the bathroom just brushed his teeth and splashed water on his face. When he returned to the living room, Mahina was already there folding up his bedding before tackling breakfast.

"Mahina, I was going to get that," he said, trying to be as less of a nuisance as possible.

"Don't worry about it, chile. I got it." She glanced over her shoulder at him. "Ain't you got something to do today?"

Hylan opened his mouth.

"Said he's been thinking," Lathan volunteered, cutting him off.

"Shouldn't be much to think about," Mahina said. "Everybody knows what you need to do."

Hylan opened his mouth again.

"That's what I told him," Lathan chuckled as he poured his first cup of coffee.

"Everybody doesn't know all the facts," Hylan said, making his way to the kitchen and the coffeemaker.

"I know that it's time to stop playing house and make an honest woman out of that girl. Do I need to bop you over the head with my skillet to knock some sense into you?"

"Uh-huh," Lathan cosigned.

Hylan almost dropped the carafe. "What? You know?"

The husband and wife looked at each other before Mahina said, "We're old—not dumb."

"But—but, I don't understand." Hylan sat down at the table. "How long have you known?"

Mahina shrugged. "I've known for about a week after meeting the girl. But she seemed nice and harmless. Then after getting to know her a bit better, I just figured that she was just a woman who was down on her luck. She turned out to be a great li'l helper around the property. I could use it, you know. These old bones aren't what they used to be."

"Speak for yourself," Lathan said, leaning back and jamming a finger through his tool belt. "There's not a damn thing I can't do now that I didn't do when I was twenty-five."

One of Mahina's brows hiked up.

Lathan coughed and then amended, "Well, almost everything."

Hylan chuckled and then tried to wrap his head

around this latest news. "So…does that mean everybody knows?"

Mahina looked insulted. "What? I don't be spreading everything I know. I believe most people just took her at her word. When they saw how big her heart was, they fell in love with her." Her gaze shifted to her husband. "I guess Lathan and I were hoping that you would, too."

"So you let me carry on with this shenanigan for the past three months?"

Mahina laughed. "I don't recall seeing no gun put to your head. You did what you wanted to do…like always."

There was no point arguing with that. Mahina was telling the truth. "Well, her father certainly believes that we're married…and that I've been cheating on her with Shonda for the whole time she was here. He still wouldn't let me see her or let her take any of my calls."

"And he still hasn't put her on no plane," Mahina countered. "I imagine a father like Nikki's would have done some investigating long before he showed up and discovered that there was no marriage license. Have you personally gone over there and tried to talk to her?"

"You're right." A smile stretched across Hylan's face as he jumped up from the table. "Mahina, you're a genius…and an angel!"

"Of course I am. Everybody knows that."

Hylan planted a big kiss on the side of her face and then shouted as he raced toward the door, "Call Reverend Oxford. See if he can perform a ceremony today. I'm getting married!"

* * *

"What's taking him so damn long?" Wilbur huffed, walking around the kitchen in circles with a cup of coffee in his hand.

Ella sighed as she flipped bacon over in the skillet. "Maybe you shouldn't have punched him, Wilbur. You got the man scared to come to his own house."

Wilbur waved the comment off. "Are you kidding me? The man had an iron jaw. It damn near broke my hand."

Ella shook her head. "You know what I mean."

Wilbur shook his head, not willing or ready to consider that he may have botched things up. But when he could feel his wife's heavy stare, he conceded a bit. "Okay. Maybe I did get a little carried away, but I had to make it look good, didn't I?"

Ella shook her head. "I told you we should just let things take their natural course. It was clear from the moment we met him that he was crazy about Nikki. And she him, I might add. She just has this natural glow about her now. If I didn't know any better, I'd think that..." Ella glanced up at the ceiling as if she could see through the floor and into the master bedroom.

Wilbur frowned. "You'd think what?"

She returned her attention to her husband and pushed up a smile. "Nothing, dear."

He shrugged and continued his pacing. "Kappa Psi Kappa men usually go after what they want. I would have thought he'd show up sooner, demanding to see his wife."

"They're not married."

"Well, you know what I mean."

Ella shook her head. "The sad part is that I do."

"I expect him to storm over here and fight for her. Not just try to call her on the phone."

"It takes men a minute to admit that they're in love," Ella said. "Especially you Kappa Psi Kappa men."

The first smile of the morning twitched at the corners of Wilbur's mouth.

The Jamisons had known for quite some time that their daughter wasn't married. After Barbara delivered the news two years ago, it took less than twenty-four hours and a cheap detective to uncover the truth. But Ella had insisted on giving their daughter some space to work out whatever it was that she needed to work out after failing so badly with her last play. But when the months rolled into years, she feared that her daughter was considering not returning home.

Their vacation trip was really supposed to be an intervention of sorts to get Nikki to see reason and return home. They were all surprised to see Hylan Dawson and were further thrown off guard by the undeniable affection between the couple.

"He's gotta love her," Wilbur said. "Why else was he playing along with that ridiculous charade?"

"He said he loved her," Ella agreed.

"Right." He snapped his fingers. "And let's not forget that he offered to pay back that investment. If that wasn't a sign of love I don't know what is."

Ella started preparing him a plate. "Don't worry, Wilbur. He should be along soon."

Chapter 19

Derrick, Charlie, Taariq and Stanley all gripped the sides of Rafiq's compact four-wheeler with fear in their hearts while their short thirty-five years flashed before their eyes. They had all hesitated when the chatty driver had first whipped up on the airport tarmac and nearly ran them over, but after he'd mentioned that he and his aunt worked at Hylan's vacation home, they all figured "what the hell?" Now hell was exactly what they were going through as Rafiq kept his heavy foot jammed down against the accelerator.

"I gotta tell you that's it been nothing but drama since Mr. Dawson returned home. The gossip grapevine has never been busier."

"Is that right?" Taariq shouted above the G-force that was trying to rip him from his seat.

"Yep. To tell the truth, me and the missus thought he was never gonna come back. Figured he and his wife was going through some kind of trouble."

"His wife?" Derrick asked.

"I told you," Taariq said. His boys thought he'd been joking after his phone call to the house.

"And who exactly is his wife?" Stanley asked, looking whiter than usual.

Rafiq frowned. "Why Nikki, of course. Everybody knows Nikki."

The Kappa men exchanged looks before Taariq said, "Not everybody."

"How long have they been married?" Charlie questioned.

Rafiq shrugged. "Don't know exactly, but I believe it's something like two years."

"TWO YEARS!" they all thundered.

Rafiq jumped and jerked the steering wheel.

The men yelled—but Stanley's stood out more like a high-pitch scream.

"It's okay. It's okay," Rafiq assured, swerving the vehicle back into the right lane. "You guys should not scare me like that."

"*Scare* you?" Taariq asked. "Have you ever thought about driving a little slower than a rocket?"

Rafiq laughed. "Aw. Don't worry I'm a very good driver. I haven't had an accident all summer."

"That's comforting," Stanley said.

Rafiq glanced back in his rearview mirror at Stanley. "Hey, are you okay? No throwing up inside my car."

"I'll try to keep that in mind," Stanley croaked.

"So tell us a little more about Hylan's wife," Derrick said.

Rafiq smiled and rattled off all that he knew about Soufrière's adopted angel and then all that had transpired since Hylan showed up back in June.

"Her father laid Hylan out?" Taariq choked back a laugh.

Rafiq shrugged. "To my man's defense, I think the punch caught him off guard."

"They usually do," Charlie said.

Stanley was shaking his head. "I just don't get it. None of this sounds like Hylan. He wouldn't have kept something like this from us." He glanced to his brothers. "Would he?"

Taariq shook his head. "Nah. And I don't see him inviting Shonda down here if he had a wife tucked away."

"If you ask me none of this is making any damn sense," Derrick said.

Rafiq shrugged. "I'm just telling you what I know. If things continued the way they are right now I don't think the Dawsons will be married for long—especially if her father has any say about it."

"Hey, isn't that Hylan running up there?" Stanley asked, pointing to a figure racing along the road.

Before anyone could blink they had caught up with the man.

"Stop the car," Taariq yelled. To which Rafiq obeyed immediately and damn near threw everyone out of the car.

Hylan dove out of the way when he saw the Jeep

fishtail and was about to clip him. "What the hell?!" He hit the ground so hard that for a moment he wondered if he had the ability to sit back up.

"Hylan, man. Is that you?"

He popped his head up. "Taariq?" Glancing over at the Jeep that nearly killed him, he saw his four Kappa brothers and Rafiq all squished up in the front seat.

"Yo, man. Get off me," Derrick complained.

"I'm trying," Charlie said, scrambling to return to the back seat.

Hylan winced as he stumbled to his feet. "Hey, what are you guys doing here?" He limped over to the Jeep.

"Thinking of new and eventful ways to kill ourselves, apparently," Taariq responded, cutting an angry glare at their driver.

"We came out here to find out what the hell was going on," Derrick corrected. "What's this shit about you being married?"

Rafiq leaned forward to catch Hylan's answer.

"You know what, guys. It's a long story, but move over so I can catch a ride back to my crib."

Rafiq's smile bloomed. "Ah, finally going to go get you the missus back, eh?"

"You're damned right." He climbed in and forced the brothers to make room. "How do you guys feel about attending a wedding this afternoon?"

"Ah. Thinking about renewing your vows?" Rafiq concluded.

Hylan smiled. "I guess you can say that."

* * *

"Mom, Dad, there's something I have to tell you," Nikki began, standing in the kitchen. She'd been practicing this speech for the last two days and after running it by her baby sister the night before, she knew that it was now time to tell her parents the truth. "It's about me and Hylan."

Her parents shared a look at each other and then reached for each other's hand at the table.

"You see, um, Hylan and I…" Her eyes misted. "We're not exactly…um."

After a long silence, her father helped her out. "Married," he said.

Nikki's head sprung up, her face contorted with confusion. "You know?"

"Of course we knew, sweetheart," her mother said gently. "We may be getting old but we're not stupid."

"I-I never meant to suggest…" She glanced at her sister. "How long have you known?"

"Shortly after you told us you'd gotten married," her mother said.

"Why didn't you tell me," she asked Barbara.

"We were waiting for you to come forward with the truth. We came to get you to come back home, but then we met Hylan."

Her mother jumped in. "And saw how much he cared for you. So then we thought we had it all wrong."

Nikki shook her head. "I think I need to sit down." Barbara helped her over to a chair. "But Daddy, you punched him."

Wilbur shifted uncomfortably in his chair. "Yeah,

well. I like the boy and all, but he did tell me to shut the hell up."

"I don't believe this," Nikki said.

"Oh, baby. He'll calm down," her mother said. "His pride is just wounded."

"You think? We kicked the man out of his own house."

His father chuckled. "Yeah, that is classic." When he realized that no one else was laughing, he sobered up. "Baby, why did you do it?"

Nikki huffed out a long tired breath. "Believe it or not, it sounded like a good idea at the time."

"That's what scares me," her father lamented.

"Wilbur," Ella chided.

"It's true," Wilbur insisted. "Nikki, you've got to learn to control some of this impulsiveness. Now, I know that the play's failure really affected you and I'm sorry if I played a part in making you feel like you couldn't come to talk to any of us about it. You can't run away from your problems. You have to learn to face them."

Tears leaked and then poured down her face. "But I've made such a mess of everything. I don't know if I can fix this one."

"Sure you can," Barbara said, forever the one lending an encouraging word. "We'll be right here helping you."

Nikki smiled at the unconditional love radiating from her sister's eyes. "Have I told you lately that you're the best sister anyone could ever have?"

Barbara's face lit up. "No. But I think that honor belongs to you."

The two sisters embraced.

Outside, a horn blared. Once. Twice. And then a long final one.

"Nikki!"

Nikki's head popped up as she released Barbara. "Hylan?"

"Well, it's about damn time," Wilbur mumbled under his breath as he pushed back from the table.

"Nikki!"

"Wilbur, now don't ruin this," Ella warned, jumping up and following him as he stormed toward the door.

"Daddy, don't." Nikki rushed out of her chair. Her mind was swirling at the fact that Hylan was there. Had he come to finally kick them out of his house? She couldn't blame him.

"Don't worry," Wilbur said as he marched toward the door. "I got this under control."

Nikki didn't like the sound of that. "Daddy, please don't hit him again."

"I won't."

"Nikki!"

"Promise?" she asked her father.

"I promise." He whipped open the front door. "Now what is all this hollering about out here?" Wilbur thundered and jabbed his fists into his sides.

Hylan climbed over Charlie and Derrick, stomping on a few feet and laps in the process, and jumped out of the Jeep. "I came to get my wife," he declared.

Wilbur's brows shot up. "Is that right?"

"Yeah. That's right," he said, strolling confidently up the front stairs. "Regardless of what anybody thinks

I've done or haven't done, I love your daughter and I'm *not* about to let her go."

Nikki gasped in disbelief. Surely she wasn't hearing him right.

"What if I say that it's not up to you?" Wilbur challenged.

"Then I'd tell you that it's not up to you, either, Mr. Jamison," Hylan countered and then looked past Wilbur's shoulder to lock gazes with Nikki. "This is between me and Nikki. And I came here to ask her to marry me…again."

The women gasped.

"What?" Wilbur thundered.

But Hylan swore he saw a smile tug at the man's lips. "With your permission, of course."

Wilbur turned to stare at his daughter. "Is this something that you want?"

Nikki was completely and utterly speechless. "I… I…"

"We could do it today. Mahina is calling the reverend."

Oh, my God. He's serious.

"I know that this is all short notice," he said, moving past Wilbur to stand in front of Nikki. "But I've always been a man who believed in living in the moment. And at this moment, I know that I have *never* felt this way about anyone before. I know that I can make you happy. I know I can protect you. And I know that I will never ever stop loving you."

Nikki's hand fluttered to her open mouth.

"Nicole Dawson," Hylan said, slowly dropping to

one knee. "Will you do me the honor of becoming my wife…for real this time?"

Nikki dropped her hands and shouted without hesitation, "yes!"

From the Jeep, Stanley wiped at his eyes. "That has to be the most beautiful thing I've ever seen." He sniffled. "I just wish that I understood it."

"You're not the only one," Taariq said, patting him on the back.

"Sounds like it doesn't matter, guys," Derrick chirped. "It looks like we're headed for a wedding."

Epilogue

Two hours later...

Word of the Dawsons renewing their marriage vows spread through Soufrière faster than the Great Fire of Chicago. Only a handful of people knew that this would in fact be the first time the couple would be exchanging vows, but it seemed like such a small matter to correct that no one really tried. Obtaining a license took about as long as it did to drive through the Little White Chapel in Las Vegas.

While Nikki rushed to get dressed, her close-knit family kept asking whether she was sure that this was what she really wanted. They liked Hylan but for parents, the rush was a legitimate concern. But Nikki had never been more sure of anything in her entire life. When her father and mother left to go scramble and get ready, Barbara pulled her sister to the side and asked, "Don't you think you should tell Hylan about the baby?"

"Don't worry. By my estimations, I still have a good seven months to tell him," Nikki laughed. She felt positively giddy. She was about to be married—for real this time. Speaking of which, she pulled the small diamond band off her hand and tossed it into the small wooden jewelry box on top of the bedroom dresser. "Guess I won't be needing that anymore."

Barbara frowned. "By the way, where did you get that ring?"

"Pawn shop. Fifty bucks. Bought it in the Castries quarter so no one here would know."

"Maybe I should be asking whether Hylan knows what he's getting into with you," Barbara said, shaking her head.

"After three months together, I think he may have some idea." She turned and faced her sister. "How do I look?"

Barbara clasped her hands together as tears glossed her soft brown eyes. "Beautiful."

Nikki glanced down at her simple, white cotton dress and low-heeled shoes. "It's nothing fancy, but it'll do." She took a deep breath. "Oh, Barbara. I can't believe I'm about to get married. Hell, we haven't even discussed where we'll live."

"I hope it'll be New York."

"Could be Atlanta," Nikki said.

"Or it could be here," Barbara suggested and then cocked her head. "Does it matter to you?"

Nikki took less than a second to think about it. "Absolutely not. I'll go wherever he wants me to go."

A side of Barbara's mouth quirked up. "Now that sounds like the right answer to me." She strolled over to her sister and swept her into a big embrace. "I'm so proud of you, sis."

Nikki teared up. "I swear," she said, shaking her head. "Once upon a time I never thought I'd hear you say that." She sniffed and tried her best not to ruin her makeup.

Momma Mahina poked her silver head inside the room. "Reverend Oxford is here. Ten minutes?"

"Sounds good," Nikki released her sister and drew in a deep breath.

Momma Mahina smiled and pushed on into the room. "Let me steal one of those hugs, chile."

"Absolutely."

Mahina beamed as she shuffled her way over. When she enfolded Nikki into her arms, she squeezed her tight. Anyone would have thought that one of her own children were about to get married. One thing was for sure, Nikki was definitely feeling the love. "Hmm, hmm, hmm. It's been a long road," Mahina said as she pulled back. "Knowing Hylan as I do and for as long as I have, I can truly say I never thought this day would come, but I'm glad that it has."

Confused, Nikki's brows nearly crashed together.

Momma Mahina winked. "Take care of each other.

Given how you two met, I'd say this union had a lot to do with destiny."

Nikki cocked her head as she watched the older woman shuffle out the room. Then she started laughing. "You knew," she said with sudden clarity.

Mahina winked and smiled. "Like I told Hylan, I'm old, but I'm not stupid."

"But how…why did you…?"

"None of that matters a lick now, does it?" she said. "All that matters is that it all turned out right in the end. Now I'll see you downstairs. You and that bun you got in the oven."

In a guest room down the hall, Hylan tried to supply his Kappa brothers with the 4-1-1 on how he met his wife, well, his soon-to-be wife. But every other sentence was cut off with one of them asking him to run something by them again.

"You mean to tell me that she was up here frontin'?" Taariq said after finally picking his jaw up off the floor. "Who the hell does that?"

"I know it all sounds a little odd. But—"

"A little odd?" he thundered. "Try crazy as hell."

Derrick drew a deep breath and settled a hand on Taariq's shoulder. "Calm down."

"Calm down? Are you for real?" Taariq said. "Our man has either got caught slippin' or has lost his mind. Either way, it ain't good."

"I don't know," Charlie said. "He looks pretty sane to me. He's just in love."

"Figures. Your mind ain't been right since you met

your wife, Gisella." Taariq huffed out a long breath and rolled his eyes.

Derrick opened his mouth.

"And don't you say nothing because you're the one that set off this whole domino effect." Taariq started to look misty eyed. "How could you guys do this to a brother?" He shook his head and started pounding his chest. "I thought we were boys. We were supposed to ride this bachelorhood thang until the wheels came off. Playas for life. Remember that? Now look at y'all. Make me the last brother standing and everything."

Stanley moved forward. "Hey, man. You're not alone out here. You know you always got me."

Taariq pursed his lips together and just gave the other brothers a look that said "see what y'all done left me with?"

Hylan laughed. "Look man, I know what you're saying. I was talking that same crap just a few months ago."

"Ah, yeah." Charlie bobbed his head. "Guess you waved that white flag of surrender, too, Mr. It's-Never-Gonna-Happen."

Hylan threw up his hands. "All right. All right. I deserved that one." He chuckled at all that mess he was talkin' just a few short months ago. "Just charge it all to the game I guess, because I'm marrying Nikki *today*."

Taariq shook his head and mumbled, "It just ain't right."

Derrick glanced over at Charlie. "You know Isabella

and Gisella are going to be mad that they missed out on a Caribbean wedding."

Charlie shook his head. "True. But Gisella is too far along in her pregnancy to fly anyway. At least that's the excuse I'm gonna lay on her."

"Hmm. Well I'm going to direct all Isabella's complaints straight to the man who's responsible for this sudden rush."

"Send her my way," Hylan said. "I got this."

There was a knock on the door.

"Come in," Hylan yelled.

Mahina pushed open the door and stuck her head inside. "The reverend is here. Think you guys can be ready in five minutes?"

"I'm ready now." Hylan puffed out his chest.

His boys laughed at his eagerness.

"Damn, man." Taariq slapped a hand against Hylan's back. "My bad. You really are sprung."

Smiling, Hylan shrugged his friend's hand off his back. "All right. Keep poppin' that B.S. That just tells me that your ass is gonna be next."

Taariq's hands shot up in the air. "Now don't try putting no hexes on a brotha. I ain't puffing on whatever it is y'all puffing on."

"Then I'll be next," Stanley declared.

All eyes turned toward him.

"Are you even seeing anybody?" Derrick asked.

"Bump that. When was the last time you had a date?" Charlie razzed.

Stanley puffed out his thin chest and waved his

brothers off. "C'mon now. Y'all know I gets the ladies."

They all gave him the "get real" stare.

"A'ight. A'right," Stanley said, determined not to pay them no mind. "Watch. I'm gonna find me a honey so fly, y'all gonna be trippin' over your tongues."

Derrick winced. "Honey?"

"Fly?" Charlie asked.

"See that's your problem right there," Taariq said. "You're still lost in the '90s. Just be happy that Tawanda over at the Waffle House takes pity on you and breaks you off a piece every once in a while."

They all cracked up laughing.

"All right. We better get ready to do this." Hylan said and then remembered something. "By the way, I got this business venture I want y'all to take a look at soon."

They all looked confused at Hylan's seemingly sudden change of subject.

"My baby girl wrote this cool play and I want you guys to consider investing in it."

Once again, the men exchanged looks. "All right, man," Derrick said, holding up his fist and giving his man dabs. "You got it."

Hylan beamed as each one cosigned on the deal. Instinct told him that finding backers for his bride's next play was the best wedding present he could ever offer her.

Two minutes later, Hylan and the Kappa men pushed and squeezed their way through a packed house. The moment the guests realized the groom was coming through, a sudden cheer went up and they finally started moving out of the way.

"Damn. Is everybody in the Caribbean in here?" Taariq grumbled.

"Trust me. They're here for my wife," Hylan chuckled. "They're crazy about her."

And it was true because the little whoop that Hylan had created was nothing compared to the full-out cheer that went up when Nikki and her small entourage made their way down the aisle before the smiling reverend.

"I guess you weren't kidding," Taariq whispered.

Hylan didn't hear a word his brother was saying. His eyes were locked on the prize walking toward him. She was still the most beautiful thing he'd ever seen. It didn't matter that they weren't dropping a mint on an over-the-top ceremony where she could rock a one of a kind couture gown. She could never be more breathtaking than she was right now.

When she finally stopped to stand by his side, Hylan's chest ached from the beauty of this special moment. Truth be told, he didn't hear much of what Reverend Oxford was saying, either. All he could do was just marvel at the woman that he was about to call wife—well, for real this time. He didn't know what the future held, but he knew for sure that he was going to love her for the rest of their days and that with her quirky personality, there would never be a dull moment in their lives.

"I do," she said smiling.

A moment later, it was Hylan's turn. "I do."

"With the power vested in me, I now pronounce you

husband and wife." Reverend Oxford slapped his Bible closed. "You may now kiss the bride."

Hylan leaned in and sealed their lives together with a kiss that would be seared in his memory forever.

Everyone in the house roared with applause and a second later the bride and groom were literally bumrushed by their guests with handshakes, hugs and kisses. After seeing her sister being jerked from one embrace to another, Barbara panicked and took on the role of bodyguard.

"Careful, careful. The woman is pregnant!" Realizing what she'd just said, Barbara gasped and slapped both hands over her mouth.

And just like that a hush fell over the crowd. Hylan stood staring at his wife, mouth open.

Nikki timidly hunched her shoulders up. "Surprise, honey."

Charlie reached over and waved his hand before his friend's eyes to make sure that he was still with them. "I think you're supposed to say something," he whispered.

Hylan pumped his fists straight into the air. "Yeah, baby! Victory!" He rushed over and swooped his wife up into his arms and spun her around.

Nikki squealed and then found herself smothered in the sweetest kiss she'd ever known.

* * * * *

REQUEST YOUR FREE BOOKS!

2 FREE NOVELS
PLUS 2 FREE GIFTS!

Love's ultimate destination!

KROM10R

THE *MATCH MADE* SERIES

**Melanie Harte's exclusive matchmaking service—
The Platinum Society—can help any soul find their
ideal mate. Because when love is perfect,
it is a match made in heaven...**

Book #1
by *Essence* Bestselling Author
ADRIANNE BYRD
Heart's ♡ Secret
June 2010

Book #2
by National Bestselling Author
CELESTE O. NORFLEET
Heart's ♡ Choice
July 2010

Book #3
by *Essence* Bestselling Author
DONNA HILL
Heart's ♡ Reward
August 2010

www.kimanipress.com
www.myspace.com/kimanipress

L♥VE IN THE LIMELIGHT

Fantasy, Fame and Fortune...Hollywood-Style!

Book #1
By *New York Times* and *USA TODAY*
Bestselling Author Brenda Jackson

STAR OF HIS HEART
August 2010

Book #2
By A.C. Arthur

SING YOUR PLEASURE
September 2010

Book #3
By Ann Christopher

SEDUCED ON THE RED CARPET
October 2010

Book #4
By *Essence* Bestselling Author Adrianne Byrd

LOVERS PREMIERE
November 2010

Set in Hollywood's entertainment industry,
two unstoppable sisters and their two friends
find romance, glamour and dreams-come-true.

KIMANI™
ROMANCE

www.kimanipress.com
www.myspace.com/kimanipress